About the author

Richard Glover is the author of nine books, including the bestsellers *In Bed with Jocasta* and *The Dag's Dictionary*. He writes a weekly column for the *Sydney Morning Herald* and presents the Drive show on ABC Radio in Sydney.

desperate husbands

Richard Glover

HarperCollins*Publishers*

HarperCollins_Publishers_

First published in Australia in 2005
by HarperCollins_Publishers_ Australia Pty Limited
ABN 36 009 913 517
www.harpercollins.com.au

HarperCollins_Publishers_
25 Ryde Road, Pymble, Sydney, NSW 2073, Australia
31 View Road, Glenfield, Auckland 10, New Zealand
77–85 Fulham Palace Road, London, W6 8JB, United Kingdom
2 Bloor Street East, 20th floor, Toronto, Ontario M4W 1A8, Canada
10 East 53rd Street, New York NY 10022, USA

National Library of Australia Cataloguing-in-Publication data:

Glover, Richard.
    Desperate Husbands.
    ISBN 0 7322 8250 0.
    1. Glover, Richard – Family – Humor. 2. Family – Humor.
    3. Husbands – Humor. I. Title.
306.850207

Cover design and illustrations by Katherine Hall, De Luxe & Assoc.
Cover and internal design by Natalie Winter, HarperCollins Design Studio
Author photograph by Paul Henderson
Typeset in 12/16 Goudy by Kirby Jones
Printed and bound in Australia by Griffin Press on 50gsm Bulky News

5 4 3 2 1   05 06 07 08

For Amanda Higgs

contents

Acknowledgements

The author would like to thank Debra Oswald; Dan and Joe Glover; Tony Scullion and Peter Harrison from the *Sydney Morning Herald*; Nellie Flannery and Annabelle Sheehan from RGM; Sascha Rundle, Rory Macdonald and Laura Bailey from the ABC; and, from HarperCollins, Linda Funnell, Shona Martyn and Mary Rennie.

Introduction

A decade or so ago, I invented a game called *Who's Got the Weirdest Parents?*. It's true it didn't receive the rush of global attention achieved by Trivial Pursuit or Su Doku, but among my small group of friends, it became mildly popular for at least a few months.

The rules were simple enough. A group of people would gather in a circle, armed with a bottle of wine or two, and take turns recounting weird stories about their parents or, in some versions, their extended family. Within minutes you'd hear stories of such total frothing insanity, you'd be left gasping for breath. How could your seemingly normal friends have clambered out of such a murky genetic pool?

Why did I invent the game? All my life I have been hopeless at games, both physical and intellectual. My earliest memory of school is of a rugby coach barking at me, 'Go get the ball, Glover,' and me calling back in an effete trill, 'Can't, sir. Might get hurt, sir.' I had a vested interest in developing a game in which I had some chance of victory. *Who's Got the Weirdest Parents?* was surely that game.

When I was a baby, growing up in New Guinea, my mother had wrapped stickytape around my head in a failed attempt to reduce the angle of my protruding ears. She only stopped when the district nurse asked about the cause of the bloodied stripe around my infant skull. Tropical heat rash? No, stickytape trauma. My father, as a young British sailor, had visited Hiroshima a few weeks after the dropping of the bomb and had long been convinced that only by drinking heavily could he keep the radioactive effects at bay.

By the time I was fifteen, their marriage was such that my mother ran off with my school English teacher. This left my fellow students so gobsmacked it took them as long as a week to realise that, in a situation like this, it was their job to taunt me mercilessly. My father, meanwhile, was so heartbroken that he left home as well — rushing back to England and leaving me the house.

I'm not complaining: it was a pleasant middle-class suburban home. It even had a pool and a chest freezer. But the truth remains — as Jocasta, my partner, sometimes puts it — 'Richard never really left home. Home left him.'

My father eventually returned home, yet this story — complete with Jocasta's one-liner — was often enough to push me over the line to victory in *Who's Got the Weirdest Parents?* But sometimes not. What was amazing was that everybody had a story. At least one of their parents, on at least one occasion, had done something truly bizarre.

One friend, for example, explained how her father, a medical practitioner, would sit in front of the TV each night with a pillow tied to his head, sucking on a hanky. It was his method of reducing the poisonous messages emanating from the TV set. Another recounted how his father would walk around the house naked, singing love songs to a mistress who may or may not have existed — no one in the family could be sure.

'OK,' we'd all say at that point. 'Game over. You win.'

On some occasions, a friend might explain that they were unable to play. 'It sounds like good fun,' they would say, 'but I'll sit this one out and listen. You see, my parents where so staid, boring and normal . . . '

They'd just be finishing this last bit of the sentence — 'staid, boring and normal' — when they'd start to slow down, as if walking through sticky mud. The last word would come out like a slowed-down tape-recording: 'and n-o-r-m-a-l.' There would then be this troubled pause, followed by the words: 'Well, unless you count the way my father . . . '

Out would then tumble some eye-popping tale of total barking madness, made more remarkable by the fact that the family had clearly become so completely used to it they no longer saw it as odd.

I remember in particular an old flatmate who spent five minutes apologising for his crushingly dull parents and his consequent inability to play the game, before being hit by a sudden thought.

'Well,' he said after a pause, 'unless you count the way my father couldn't bear the thought of anyone else touching or laundering his clothes. He installed a washer and a dryer, right there in the garage, so that he could come home from work, park the car, and then personally do all the laundering and drying of his work clothes before entering the house.

They'd then be ready to slip on again before he drove out in the morning without anyone else having touched them.

'Would a story like that count in the game?'

'Yeah,' someone would say after a stunned silence. 'That's generally the sort of thing we would count.'

One of the things I like about the TV show *Desperate Housewives* is that it acknowledges how bizarre life can get in the suburbs. I've only one complaint about the show. The producers should realise: it's not only the housewives who are desperate.

None of the Desperate Housewives has a mother as insane as mine — a mother who routinely cleans her son's appliances to death. Not one is shacked up with someone as fabulous and fierce as my partner, Jocasta — a woman whose mood changes according to whatever novel she happens to be reading. And not one is as mad as me, for reasons that will become apparent.

In the end, why should the Desperate Housewives be quite so desperate? They're rich, good-looking and very thin. Their appliances all work. They have time to apply lip gloss.

If you want to know *desperate*, just come this way . . .

desperate

Things are getting desperate. I must try and re-engage her with reality. I shout out to her: 'Do you know where the shin-guards are? Did we ever get them out of the car from last week?' To which she responds: 'In Moscow the trees on the boulevards are in leaf, and dust rises from the roads.'

The revolt of the appliances

For the first time in ages our bank account has struggled into the serious black. At one point there's a couple of thousand bucks in there, uncommitted cash, just sitting about, winking at me. I feel like Kerry Packer. I begin contemplating all sorts of rash behaviour: paying off loans, adding to my super, buying a pair of jeans without a big hole in the crotch. It's a moment of liberation. Which is when every appliance in our house drops dead. Fridge, oven, video and dryer. It is as if they were signalling to each other: 'Quick, the bastard is about to get ahead. Let's do something. Everyone together now: die.'

All the appliances go within ten days of each other. Not one appliance can be fixed. All need to be replaced. We are now heavily in debt. Mr Bung Lee and Mr Hardly Normal are both a lot richer.

First to go is the fridge. Suddenly, in the middle of the night, it emits a low, straining growl, like that of a wounded animal. Apparently, fridges always die in the middle of the night. I guess they are alone in their task of crisping the vegetables and fall victim to existential dread. 'What's it all for?' whines the fridge. 'What's in it for me?'

By morning the corpse is already warm. A pool of dirty water spreads over the floor, like a bloodstain in a Tarantino movie. Due to my mass-manufacturing cooking methods, I am staring at my own body weight in defrosted bolognaise sauce.

'I am staring at my own body weight in defrosted bolognaise sauce,' I say to Jocasta.

'Don't exaggerate,' says Jocasta, bleakly. 'There'd only be 100 kilos in there, max.'

I find her comments insulting, and so distract myself with the *Yellow Pages*. The Fridge Man is called. He arrives and declares there is no hope.

I set out on my first trip to Mr Bung Lee. It's twenty years since I have bought a fridge and things have changed. The fridges all have ice-makers, water dispensers and, in one case, internet access. This, presumably, is so the fridge can better access your banking details, and time the perfect moment to stop working.

One model even records the pattern of your fridge usage, turning up the cold during periods in which you habitually open the door: in my case, the half-hour between 9.30 and 10.00 every night, during which I simply cannot believe we have run out of beer. I open the fridge, root around, close the fridge, sigh and then open the door once more. Surely, if I just check once more behind the cabbage, a final beer will suddenly appear?

Jocasta has noted this behaviour and thinks less of me for it. I already live with a contemptuous woman. I'm unsure whether I also want to live with a contemptuous fridge. I go for the simplest model. They deliver it two days later.

Just when the new fridge arrives, the oven decides to stop working: it seems that the appliances are involved in some sort of tag-team relay. The oven, mind you, has never really worked, which may be why we've spent the last fifteen years living on a diet of unrelieved bolognaise sauce. Now it's given up all signs of life. Frankly, I'm glad the mongrel is dead. I remove more money from the bank account and pay a visit to Mr Hardly Normal. I buy the oven with the biggest discount sticker — an insanely complex wall unit, featuring twenty-three different combinations of bottom element, top element, fans and grills. I try to get Jocasta on the phone to discuss the choice, but she's in a meeting. I buy it anyway, without consultation. I should be awarded an Australian Bravery Medal.

As it happens, Jocasta quite likes the oven, largely on the basis that, after fifteen years of the other one, it has the advantage of getting hot. For us, this is a remarkably novel feature in an oven.

The remaining appliances sense the happy mood. We have a new fridge, purring away, and an oven capable of getting hot. There is still money in the bank: around fifty cents, if you must ask. Jocasta even has her arm around me, and is suggesting we open a delightful bottle of white wine — as chilled by our new fridge.

The appliances panic. Their plan is in pieces. That night, the VCR eats three tapes, spitting the chewed remains venomously onto the carpet. The air is rent with the screams of the dryer, writhing like a dying wildebeest. I glance up and spot the toaster watching us, malevolently. It's then the appliances bring in the big guns. The computer seizes up.

The next morning, I ring the local computer store and arrange a home visit from one of the young technicians. I've never met him before but he has the same manner as every computer help guy I have ever met. Whether at home or work, they always walk in with the calm, avuncular manner of a senior surgeon. 'Let's see what's going wrong here,' they say with a patronising smile, as if you're a bit dim and have probably forgotten to turn the thing on at the power point. Three hours later they are still sitting there. There's some strange problem, they explain, which they are unable to identify. It's never happened before. Usually this is a ten-minute job. But not this time. They just can't figure it out.

Trouble is, there's always some strange problem. It's never a ten-minute job. They are always baffled.

This particular nineteen-year-old is now going through the items in My Computer, and clicking OK on each. It's the fifth time he's done this — pulling up the items, and clicking OK. Perhaps it's like a combination lock: if only he can click the OKs in the right sequence the machine will reveal its mysteries. It's the computer equivalent of a mechanic hitting the underside of your car with a stick, hoping the thing will suddenly roar back into life.

I just wish he'd admitted the truth when he first came to the door. 'Computers, sir, are a mystery.' That's how he should have begun. 'We know not what motivates them in their strange ways, nor how to guide or control their behaviour. I shall make various incantations before your machine, and I shall toggle between various items in My Computer, virtually at random, and we shall see if anything happens. I can make no promises. The whole process shall take three hours, after which I shall grow tired. I shall then leave, promising to return the next day, which is the last you shall see of me.'

That, at least, would be honest.

Why can't he just confess to his quasi-mystical role? Forget the zip-up jackets and black pants and go for the whole witchdoctor look. I'd like to see grass skirts, feathers taped to legs and a cassowary bone through the nose. Then I could have a little confidence my networking problems would be solved.

The young man is from the store which sold me the computer and its various 'plug-and-go' devices, so no way will he admit there's a bug or a problem, although some way through the third hour, he confesses it may have 'a shortcoming'. Aware he has conceded too much, he then interrogates me about the software I'm using, pointing out that his company only 'supports' certain combinations. This interrogation continues for some time, with the young man shaking his head occasionally. 'We don't support that, sir, not at all,' he says grimly, in much the same tone as William Wilberforce once declared that he didn't support slavery. I feel as if I've been caught out in some sort of unsavoury practice.

The Fridge Man never behaved like this, back in the early stages of the Revolt of the Appliances. 'Could be anything,' he'd said, as he advised us to throw out the stinking, moaning, defrosting wreck. 'Once they start to go wrong, you know, there's no end to your problems.' A fridge is much simpler than a computer, and yet this man had humility in the face of its minor complexities. If this had been the Computer Man, I'd be facing an interrogation about my fridge usage: 'You didn't put meat in the salad compartment, did you? Or packets of ham in the butter section. I'm afraid Westinghouse doesn't support that sort of thing.'

Does anybody know how computers work? Sometimes I think Bill Gates might, but even then I'm not sure. Perhaps, in that sprawling Microsoft compound in Seattle, they work on the same principles of trial and error; of opening and clicking at random. In huge rooms, technicians connect any old wires and record what happens. After 10,000 random connections, they discover they've invented Spell Check. A little later, in some corner of the vast space, there's a sudden shout of delight: an overweight technician has fallen heavily against a box of microprocessors and invented Windows XP.

Close to the end of the third hour, the nineteen-year-old finally succeeds in getting the computer going, having stumbled upon the right incantation, combined with the correct placement of the cassowary bone in his nose. He presents a bill which is staggering in its size and promptly leaves.

Together with Jocasta, I survey the house. Every appliance has collapsed and then been either replaced or repaired. The bank account is now in sharply negative territory.

I march through the kitchen and hear them muttering, planning fresh battles. 'We've got him down,' I hear the toaster mumble. 'Even we minor appliances now have the ability to tip him over the edge.' I note a power-crazed juice extractor nodding in furious agreement.

I throw a couple of slices of bread into the toaster and slam the lever down hard, then approach the juice extractor with a couple of rock-hard pears. For a moment at least, I have them on the run.

The suggestible woman

Living with a suggestible woman is a lottery. Especially if she's a big reader. For years, Jocasta's mood has been influenced by what she's been reading. These days, it tends to go a step further and she *becomes* whatever she's reading. Some nights I stumble home and find I'm living with Nigella Lawson. Other nights and it's Andrea Dworkin.

Monday and I spot Jocasta lying on the couch, looking combative yet kind of sexy. 'You, baby,' she says, 'are as sly as ten flies. Where have you been?'

I challenge her immediately. 'You've been getting into the Tennessee Williams again, haven't you?' I say, looking down at her. 'I thought we had a deal about that?'

'Well, honey, I just had myself the tiniest read. You know how fragile I've been feeling. And I can no more control those children than rule the storms of the sea.' And with that Jocasta swoons back on the couch, quietly sobbing.

I console myself with the thought: the Tennessee Williams phase might only last a couple of days. Jocasta is a fast reader. By midweek, she'll be onto something else. It could be an Elmore Leonard thriller. An Emily Brontë romance. More hopefully, a cookbook.

I quickly collect the plays, which she has left scattered on the coffee table next to an empty pitcher of mint julep. I search the shelves for something more robust. Maybe some Thea Astley or Fay Weldon. Some short stories perhaps, distilled and potent, so I can get the stuff into her real fast.

Wednesday we meet up after work and she's already found herself something new. It's a biography of the Dalai Lama: complete with tips on living a virtuous life. She reads out a few bits about restraint and tolerance and love. It's a wonderful book, she says. We head to a friend's place for dinner, me driving, and Jocasta giving directions. She notices a car with a flashing blinker. 'That fellow wants to turn into our lane. Why don't you let him?'

'Fellow'? Jocasta has never used a word like 'fellow' in her life. Jocasta's normal patois is located somewhere between a Sydney wharfie and a Chicago mobster. I slow down and let the guy slip in front of me. Jocasta rewards me with a little serene smile. 'Exercising restraint towards other road users can be a very pleasurable thing.' She gives another Buddha-like smile. 'Not that virtue needs any reward. It brings its own reward.' In the rear-vision mirror I can see my own face. I can't take much more of this. The car, for a start, has run out of sick bags.

Mind you, Jocasta is not the only one who is suggestible. I've got the same problem. Thursday and I'm halfway through an Evelyn Waugh book and am behaving like a floppy-haired aristocrat. 'Dinner, old chaps,' I yell to the old chaps. I tighten my cravat in front of the mirror, then hasten to the table. 'It's pretty good tuck tonight, by all accounts,' I say to no one in particular, the butler being unaccountably absent.

Jocasta, meanwhile, is getting into some heavy-grade Dashiell Hammett and is draped over the kitchen bench like a trash-talking blonde bombshell, looking sensational. 'What's a guy like you doing with a dame like me?' she purrs, uncrossing and then crossing her shapely legs. 'I'm nothing but a pile of leaves that just blew from one gutter to another.'

The thought strikes me: if I weren't a homosexual Brit with a teddy bear obsession, I'd really go for her.

Friday I walk in, wearing a pair of blue chinos, my muscles clearly outlined again my Buck Brothers shirt, a stain of sweat across my chest. I've been reading a lot of Pete Dexter, and I'm looking forward to sharing a meal with my woman. 'You are one gorgeous babe,' I tell her, to which she replies: 'I am alive — I guess — but how cold — I grow.'

I make myself a pledge: tomorrow I'll burn all her Emily Dickinson.

Saturday, I've shifted to a Tony Parsons book and stagger in, full of confused but rather delightful male energy. Plus a bottle of wine. Jocasta's been reading the *Sex and the City* book — the one I thoughtfully put in her briefcase the night before. She commandeers the wine and pours two glasses. I wrap an arm around her and nuzzle closer, talking in an amusing, snaggish way about our life together. This, I tell her, is the real us: me charming her with bon mots and little self-deprecating asides; her laughing girlishly, while slowly removing her clothing.

It's taken some work, and a little subterfuge, but finally we are momentarily united. I lead her to the bedroom, grateful that we are both at last on the same page.

When Sunday dawns the atmosphere has chilled. I've only just awoken after the frenzied delights of the night before, but I can see Jocasta is already reading. Inwardly I groan: it's Tolstoy. Even worse: Sunday is a pretty busy day — we've got to do the shopping, clean the house and take our two sons to their soccer matches. I cannot imagine the combination with Tolstoy will be a good one.

I ask her if she's enjoying the book, but she shooshes me. She says she's sick of having her brain full of the trivia of this family. 'Everyone else seems to manage to concentrate on one thing, so I'm concentrating on Tolstoy.'

It is a worrying development. For a start, the Tolstoy is very long. Even worse, its philosophical tone can stimulate far too much questioning in a person.

Jocasta swings herself out of bed, her eyes fixed to the book, and wanders out to the back porch. Some hours pass. I send Batboy and his younger brother, The Space Cadet, to check on her. 'She's just sitting there, Dad,' says The Space Cadet. 'Reading.'

I whisper to Batboy: 'Go ask her what time your soccer is and whether it's our turn to bring the oranges.' With the right bait, there's still a chance we'll be able to hook her back into some sort of reality. I watch Batboy as he goes out and speaks to her. It's good news. I can see she's saying something back.

'What was it?' I ask Batboy when he returns. He grimaces. 'She says Vronsky has decided to ride into St Petersburg, despite the winter snows.'

It's worse than I thought. I give The Space Cadet the empty Weetbix box so he can have a try. 'Tell her you're hungry and does she know if there's any more cereal.' I creep closer to the back door and listen into the answer. 'If the Samovar is cold,' Jocasta says to her son, 'then one must reheat it.'

I wonder what happened to my Tennessee Williams neurotic, my virtuous Tibetan and — most of all — my *Sex and the City* tart. I march out to confront her, only to find that a certain Russian weariness has overtaken her.

'Here's what it's like in my head,' she says, pausing midway through a page, her finger marking the spot. 'I'm sick of thinking about forty-seven different things at any single time. I'm sick of thinking about really trivial and pedestrian stuff, like the way both the kids need new shoes. And that we need, by tomorrow, to buy a birthday present for Bryonii. And that nobody has rung up your cousin to say we're sorry her dog died. And that the ironing has piled up so badly it's spilling out of the baskets and onto the floor. And all this is before I even start thinking about my paid work.'

In situations like these, it's important to move beyond mere sympathy and to offer some practical advice. Luckily, I've been reading some Hemingway and feel I can channel his manly and straightforward response.

'You're organising things all wrong, that's the problem,' I tell her, leaning back against the back door in a way that allows the sunlight to glance across my chiselled features. 'I'll give you an example. We could go to the shop and buy a single present for Bryonii. Or, instead, we could go and buy a whole load of children's birthday presents — say eight boys' presents and five girls' presents. Then just keep them in a box and dole them out when appropriate. Efficiency, you understand. And we should do more cooking in bulk and then freeze it for the week.'

I slap the doorjamb and offer her a reassuring smile. 'There you go — problem solved.'

She gives me a look in which all the winters of Russia seem concentrated. It has the chill of a thousand snowdrifts, combined with all the merry bonhomie of a Siberian salt mine. I decide, much like the Germans in Stalingrad in 1942, to beat a hasty retreat.

Through the back window, I see her settling down to another chapter. Things are getting desperate. I must try and re-engage her with reality. I shout out to her: 'Do you know where the shin-guards are? Did we ever get them out of the car from last week?' To which she responds: 'In Moscow the trees on the boulevards are in leaf, and dust rises from the roads.'

Even the Emily Dickinson phase was better than this. I decide to channel some Dickinson myself. 'I fret — that we will die here — if this woman — will not move.'

I'm going to have to think outside the square and embrace some radical options. The thought occurs to me: maybe she needs some time to herself. As when Tsar Alexander II freed the serfs, sometimes it's just as well to let the pressure off a little.

I round up the boys, and we stand in a tight semicircle around her. 'Give us jobs,' I say. 'We'll all do jobs. As many as you like.' The boys nod eagerly. Jocasta looks up and finally speaks, not of Tolstoy, but of home. 'It's not the doing. It's the thinking. It's the working out and the remembering. Why don't you give yourselves the jobs?' She shoots out a look in which is contained all the ice of the Arctic Circle, and all the joie de vivre of a midwinter potato famine.

The boys and I creep away. We shall not only do jobs, we shall run her a bath so she may read her book in peace. We jump into action. Or at least we try to jump into action: first we need to locate the plug, a clean towel and maybe some matches so we can light a nice-smelling candle. Also it would be useful to know exactly when soccer starts and the location of the field, so we can figure out the timing on the whole project, but the sheet is missing and the street directory is in the car and I can't find my keys.

I don't want to make any allegations, but *someone* seems to have hidden them.

With the promise of a bath, Jocasta finally comes inside. She finds the plug, and the matches, and the soccer draw, and my car keys, and then climbs into the bath, while we polish off the other jobs. We shall be self-starters: identifying and completing the tasks before we have even been told what they are.

Well, we *plan* to polish off the other jobs. To actually do them, we'll need some additional information. Such as the name of my cousin's dead dog. The age that Bryonii is turning. The location of the other street directory, since the one in my car has vanished. By the time Jocasta has finished her bath and empathised a little longer with poor, overburdened Anna Karenina, there should be quite a list with which to present her.

I shout through the door: 'Are you finished yet?'

Jocasta shouts back. 'Just a minute, if you don't mind. Here in Russia, there's a train on its way.'

Batboy Elliot

As you can imagine, Batboy's mother has been in tears. We raised our boy well. We bought him books, we took him to the theatre, we even suggested dance classes. And now this.

Jocasta was the first to come across the telltale signs in Batboy's bedroom. I told her she shouldn't have been snooping, but that issue was soon buried by the enormity of what she'd found. Crumpled in his pocket, there was an admission ticket to the rugby league. Then, in his cupboard, a banner for something called the 'West Tigers'.

'Maybe it's some sort of ecological trust, to save the Bengali tiger,' whimpered Jocasta hopefully.

'No, darling,' I said. 'We must face facts. Our son has become a rugby league supporter.'

'But where will it end?' said Jocasta, letting loose a low sob. 'I always imagined him settled down, with a DVD collection of great films and some wonderful books.' A tear trickled down her face. 'Not slumped in front of *The Footy Show*,' she said, keening.

I tried to reassure her. 'Look, a couple of experimental games of league doesn't always lead to *The Footy Show*. Let me talk to the lad.'

Do children always do the opposite of their parents? If the father works for Flick Pest Control, does the son become an entomologist? If the mother is a world-famous violinist, is the daughter naturally tone deaf? And if the parents know nothing about sport — if, like Jocasta and me, they have *zero* interest in sport — is it inevitable the children will follow rugby league, the most sport sport of all sport?

'We understand you need to rebel,' I say to Batboy later that night, 'but why not develop an interest in a sport such as ice-skating, or synchronised swimming, or even AFL? At least they're artistic.' Unbelievably, Batboy just rolls his eyes and walks off. Sometimes you just can't talk to teenagers.

In the typical movie storyline, the artistic boy is always trying to escape his sporty parents. It's never the other way around. In *Billy Elliot*, for example, the child is a ballet genius, confronting a parochial and violent father. You'll remember the harrowing scenes in which the brutish father forces Billy to learn boxing — the artistic boy clobbered as the stubborn father looks on.

If it were our family, the whole story would be in reverse. In fact, I'm thinking of making just such a film under the title *Batboy Elliot*.

Scene one opens with Batboy Elliot coming up the front steps of an inner-city house. Inside the kitchen his father is practising ballet steps with other members of his local men's group. Tofu burgers, brought by one of the men, sit ready on the benchtop. A large pot of camomile tea sits brewing nearby. The camera cuts away to Batboy Elliot nervously hiding his new boxing gloves in his bag as he comes up the hallway.

'Hi Dad, hi chaps,' he says as he walks through the kitchen, willing his voice to sound cheerful. No way does he want to get involved in another argument. Boxing and footy are Batboy Elliot's dreams. Why can't this narrow and stultifying society of inner-west trendies understand that?

Suddenly, the weedy voice of his father shoots out. 'Batboy Elliot, what's tha' on thy chin?' (Even though the father is an inner-Sydney trendy, he talks like a Lancashire coalminer for reasons that remain unclear.)

'Nothin' Da,' says Batboy, speaking, inexplicably enough, in the same north-country dialect. 'There's nowt amiss, like, Da.'

'Come 'ere, and let thy da look,' says the father, his voice thick with concern. Reluctantly, Batboy walks towards his father, who gently angles the boy's chin to the light.

'Thee 'ave a huge bruise on thy face. Ay! Thee bin boxing again!'

The two stare at each other. 'Say summat, lad,' the father gently insists, his north-country accent getting thicker the longer the scene goes on. Batboy Elliot is in agony. His father is using his 'caring and sharing' voice. Why can't he just scream and belt you, like the fathers in the movies?

'No, Da,' says Batboy finally, the camera hovering on the bruise. 'It was a ballet injury. I was trying for t' high leap, just like Baryshnikov, un hit an overhead awning.'

'I don't believe thee, lad,' the father says, a tear running down his face. 'But ahl nivver let thee down, lad. That bruise is terrible, but it's nowt that a camomile tea poultice won't fix.'

The scene that follows, in which the father uses his caring and sharing voice for three consecutive hours while the rest of father's ballet group look on with worried faces, will be considered one of the most scarifying in the history of cinema. Audiences will hide their eyes as the father lectures Batboy Elliot on the limiting nature of traditional sport, and the need for him to express, if at all possible, a wider selection of masculinities — all while dabbing tenderly at the bruises with a weak solution of camomile tea.

Viewers, though, will endure it all, just in order to see the uplifting final scenes in which Batboy Elliot's father becomes reconciled to having a sports jock for a son, finally seeing him rise to become host of *The Footy Show*, his proud parents cheering as part of the live studio audience.

And, as the final credits roll, we'll see Batboy Elliot's favourite team, the West Tigers, winning the NRL grand final. Needless to say, the film is set in the distant future and has some fantasy elements.

Buying time

It's three in the morning and I'm considering purchase of the BodyFirm ToningSystem — a complete exercise regime which does not require you to leave your couch. The BodyFirm — according to the TV ad — consists of a series of electrical pads which you place strategically about your body. These send small electrical shocks into your muscles causing them to flex with an involuntary spasm. *Voilà*. Constant and slimming exercise, all achieved while you are simultaneously eating chips and drinking beer. In the wider community, I believe they call this multi-tasking.

Even better, if you use your credit card and ring NOW NOW NOW, they send you the BodyShape belt — a sort of elasticised strap that vibrates whenever you stop sucking in your belly.

Have you noticed how some men always have their chests puffed out and their stomachs held in? Until now I'd thought they were merely pompous gits, but — a revelation — under that suit there's a vibrating girdle. I'd like to buy one — designed to hold everything in place under whatever enormous pressure. After all, I already own a pair of Levi 501s, in size thirty-six, which is operating in much the same way.

I focus back on the TV. The next advertisement offers a system of tapes through which I can learn various things WHILE ASLEEP. It makes me wonder: what if I purchased both products and left them connected all night? I could go to bed a fat, ignorant drunk, and wake up thin, gorgeous and with a working knowledge of German. *Sehr gut!*

Hope springs eternal at three in the morning, but questions do arise. I spot an advertisement for scissors, but why, exactly, would I want a pair of scissors so strong that I can cut through a pair of men's shoes? The picture shows a woman armed with the scissors. She cuts through paper, then a cardboard box, then picks up a pair of men's shoes and briskly slices off the toes. She smiles sweetly at the ease with which the task is achieved. Why does she do this? Has she caught him, the bastard who owns these shoes, sweaty and red-faced, with a twenty-year-old accounts manager perched naked on his knee? Has he stopped wearing his BodyShape girdle, and this is his wake-up call? Has he been learning Swahili at night just to annoy her? Or is she merely barking mad?

On late-night TV, conspicuous consumption has given way to *ridiculous* consumption: the purchase of goods so useless they'll need to be either hidden away or thrown away. There's the Hot Dog Maker which, completely unlike a saucepan, can heat hot dogs. There's the Bench-Top Pizza-Maker which, completely unlike an oven, can make a pizza.

And there's even a prawn shell remover which, completely unlike your fingers, can shell a prawn. Each device, the advertisers claim, is a significant advance on whatever preceded it. Indeed, hearing their claims, it is uncertain how the human race survived up to this point.

Here, for instance, is the sales pitch for the Electric Omelette Station which, completely unlike a frypan, can cook an omelette: 'Who knew frying eggs could be such a wonderfully indulgent activity?' begins the advertisement. 'Introducing the five gorgeous pieces of Electric Starr's Electric Omelette Station, designed to impress you as well as every admirer who will suddenly become interested in the art of cooking.'

A picture forms of a gaggle of people surrounding the chef, jostling to have a turn, so excited are they by the Electric Omelette Station. 'Please let me have a turn, Mum,' whines one teenage girl, as she elbows a transfixed grandfather out of the way. A sullen thirteen-year-old boy thumps aside his mesmerised aunt: 'I don't know what has come over me,' says the boy. 'Suddenly I have an all-consuming urge to cook.'

No doubt the explanation lies in the further description of the product: the electric double-burner unit features non-stick die-cast construction, on/off indicator lights, and what is described as 'a chrome finish with 24K gold-plated accents'.

Up to now I thought 'a gold-plated accent' referred to a Toorak matron bunging on a posh voice, but I now see I was mistaken. You can imagine the sort of praise the inventor must have received around the office. It takes some effort to replace a single frypan with a five-piece set — and yet still achieve the same omelette sitting on the same plate.

I make a cup of coffee and return in time for another set of ads — all of them for hair removal products. How can that be? Is Australia's problem with unwanted hair bigger than I'd imagined? Or is it the time of day that's to blame, with advertisements aimed at the after-midnight werewolf market?

I recall that a good friend of mine once purchased one of these TV offers: the SoftPluck, a hair removal system in which each hair is removed so gently 'you'll hardly notice'. This, according to my friend, was code for 'brutally wrench out each hair in turn until your eyes are streaming, and the air is rendered thick with the sound of wailing'. Which I guess is not quite as effective a sales pitch.

Certainly, a picture is forming of my fellow viewers: hairy people with memory loss problems. The MassiveMemory ad has been on about five times, the phone number flashing for minutes at a time. I wonder if they ever sell anything. Either you can remember the number and thus don't need the product. Or you need it, but haven't the foggiest who to call.

The weirdest thing is how so many products seem expressly designed for me. The SupaMop is 'especially for people who want a beautifully clean house without all that scrubbing'. That's me! I wonder how they knew. Meanwhile, the ChestFlexer is 'specifically designed for those who want to achieve the perfect body'. That sentiment is entirely mine. Frankly, it's spooky. All those who wish to achieve only moderately OK bodies, while they scrub away at their filthy surfaces, can step aside.

I start thinking about my credit card. I could make the call NOW NOW NOW. But — even without the help of MassiveMemory — thoughts of past purchases come floating back. Thoughts of products such as the FireMaker — a metal box into which one pressed wet newspaper thus producing compressed-paper bricks which were guaranteed to 'produce fuel for your fire which will save $$$ on electrical heaters'. I remember placing that order. I remember the excitement of making my first bricks. And I remember the way they stayed wet for weeks — finally forcing me to dry each brick, prior to use, in front of a blazing electrical heater, at the cost of a huge number of $$$ on my electricity bill.

I make myself yet another cup of coffee and arrive back just in time to see a new offer from Danoz Direct. It is for an electronic letter opener which takes all the effort out of opening letters. As with the automatic prawn sheller, I suddenly realise the terrible inadequacy of my own fingers. 'Don't you just hate tearing important documents as you struggle to open envelopes!' says the Danoz pitch, and straightaway I know what they mean. How often have I arrived home only to begin a half-hour tussle with the Telstra bill, a tussle which leaves the bill in shreds and me in tears, sobbing at the breakfast bar?

'Now,' continues Danoz, 'thanks to the Electronic Letter Opener, your envelopes will virtually open themselves.' I consider buying the product but am left wondering what I will do when the envelope arrives and I have no envelope opener with which to open the envelope containing the envelope opener. It's a moment of existential angst that leaves me quite dissatisfied with late-night commercial TV.

In a fit of pique, I switch to the dying moments of SBS and immediately fall into a deep slumber. When I awake I discover I am naked, forty kilos heavier, and can speak Slovenian. Now that's what I call high-impact television.

Hairy scary

'Don't come near me with that thing,' says Jocasta, from her side of the bed. 'You look like a sleazy creep. It's like a dead slug, just sitting there on your face. It makes you look disgusting.'

It's true the moustache doesn't suit me. For a start, it has somehow made my nose grow bigger. 'How is that possible?' I ask Jocasta, but she refuses to look, preferring to engage with a magazine photo essay on the actor Viggo Mortensen.

On a beach holiday, the normal order must be overturned. Women who usually don't give a damn about bikini waxing and nail polish are suddenly mad for it. Men who've spent the year meekly pruning and defoliating let their beards go wild. It's like dress-up time for grown-ups. And so I've got the mo.

It begins under the shower, halfway through shaving off a week's growth. 'I could stop right here and have a mo,' I think to myself, and there seems no reason not to. These are the liberations of the Australian beach holiday. You can slough off your workaday self at the same time you slough off your clothes. In a pair of sluggos, you could be anybody. For instance, the sort of guy who has a mo.

'What sort of guy has a mo?' I ask Jocasta, as she hovers with her magazine, chanting the word 'Viggo' in the hypnotic manner of a Sufi priest. 'A sleazy, creepy guy,' says Jocasta distractedly, as she turns the magazine to better appreciate another shot of Viggo.

I don't think she's right. As a mustachioed man, I think I'd be more decisive, more manly, stricter with myself and with the world. I'd probably drink less and be able to play sport. The question is: is it worth gaining all of the above if I also get a bigger nose?

'Do you think my nose has actually grown bigger or does it just look bigger?' I ask Jocasta, but she doesn't seem to hear me.

'What colour of nail polish do you think Viggo would like on a woman?' is all she says, rocking her magazine from side to side to better appreciate the effect of sunlight on the actor's skin.

'Pink,' I suggest. 'An actor would love something theatrical.' I'm hoping an answer from me might garner one from her; a tactic which fails to work. 'He's not just an actor, you know,' says Jocasta. 'He's also a poet, a horseman, and he speaks ten languages.'

The next day we're playing beach cricket. Jocasta is bowling, wearing bright pink nail polish on her toes. She's never worn nail polish in her life but such are the transformations of the beach. Our mate Neil whacks the ball hard, on a fast, low trajectory. I stretch to the left, wondering whether I'll miss the ball entirely as usual or instead catch it, fumble for a while, and then drop it. I look down to check the manner of my disgrace only to find the ball nestled sweetly in my hand. In a summer of sporting firsts, here's another. I've caught a cricket ball. The moustache has more power than I thought.

During the 1970s, I spent most of my leisure time trying to summon up a single chest hair on my otherwise hairless torso. I'd brace my body, shut my eyes, hold my breath and squeeze. Under this sort of pressure the usual result was an explosive fart, together with the odd ruptured pimple. But the hoped-for hair never put in an appearance.

Hair seemed to be some sort of code for masculinity. On TV, cricketers like Dennis Lillee mocked me with their ever-larger moustaches. Schoolmates would undo successive shirt buttons to reveal gorilla-like thatches. There was so much pure manliness knotted inside the bodies of my compatriots, it just kept bursting out — that seemed to be the unstated message. 'Mate, every time I have a shower, more of it grows; I just can't help myself' — *that* seemed to be what they were saying.

As a teenager whose main interests were theatre and the odd book, I needed all the masculinity I could get. Desperate, I considered pasting onto my chest a poultice of Dynamic Lifter; or, at last resort, the purchase of a chest wig. The chest wig I rejected due to the cost; the Dynamic Lifter due to the quite incredible smell.

As the seventies wore on, the hair on every bloke's head became progressively longer and less restrained. Some attempted sideburns, beards, even mutton chops. Chest hair, if it could be summoned up, was proudly displayed —

framed in the V-for-victory of a partially unbuttoned body shirt. Women, too, threw away their blades and let hair joyfully sprout from their legs and underarms. With every year that passed, the country became hairier. By 1976, it appeared the nation would soon resemble Cousin It from *The Addams Family*, with severe consequences for road safety.

Finally, through dint of effort, some time around my early twenties I achieved a small fuzz on the upper lip and just enough chest hairs to award them individual names. ('Hi Trevor', 'Hi Douglas', 'Hi Angelique'.) And now, years on, right at the end of the summer holidays, I have finally graduated to the mo — and with it the yearned-for masculinity.

Some strangers wander up and join our cricket game. They must think of me as a mustachioed man, and of Jocasta as a woman who habitually wears pink nail polish. I find this strangely appealing. One of the newcomers takes up the bat and hooks the ball skywards. It arcs up high, sits for a moment and then heads down towards me. There's an eternity in which to position myself and contemplate the catch. For me, this signals disaster: the more time I have to think about a catch, the more time my mind has to catalogue all the ways in which I'll drop it.

As the ball falls, I remember the time when I was the assistant coach of Batboy's baseball team. Steve, the coach, would put me on first base and try to teach the boys the rules of the game. 'The batter,' he'd explain, 'runs towards first base, and at the same I throw the ball — really fast and hard — towards Richard like this . . . '

There'd be a pause as they all watched the ball travel towards me.

'Yeah, OK, well let's just imagine he caught it,' Steve would say, brightly. 'If he'd caught it, that runner would then be out.'

Back at the beach, I can feel everyone watching me. Never before has a ball moved so slowly; so precisely towards a waiting fielder. It must be the easiest catch in the history of beach cricket. I scrunch up my eyes, jerk my arms into the air and feel the ball drop perfectly into my hands. 'Great catch,' someone yells. I breathe out, and give the moustache an appreciative rub. The thicker the mo gets, the more my play resembles that of a young Dennis Lillee.

'I think it's changed your personality,' says Jocasta that night, as she changes her nail polish colour to an electric sapphire blue. 'What happened to the man I shacked up with — incompetent, self-pitying, hopeless at games and unable to control his drinking? Frankly, I'd got used to that guy.'

Maybe she has a point. What sort of guy has a moustache? Not a guy like me. The mo has to go. So does her nail polish, and the magazine with Viggo. The next morning, the last day of our holidays, I shave the thing off. Almost instantly, my nose returns to its normal size. We have a final game of beach cricket with Jocasta bowling, her toes reassuringly unadorned. I take the bat, miss her first three balls, and get clean-bowled on the fourth.

The holidays are over; and so is the new me.

He used to be taller

It's my view that we should make no preparations for my mother's arrival. None at all. 'She's the one with the problem,' I tell Jocasta. 'Why should we get uptight about it?'

But Jocasta just shakes her head. 'You don't understand. The woman of the household always gets the blame. It will be on my head. Not yours.'

My mother believes we live like pigs in our own filth. She will arrive on Wednesday wearing white gloves to ward off the germs, and will insist on washing all our glassware, plates and cooking utensils before she agrees to eat anything prepared in our kitchen. During her last visit, she located the Spray n'Wipe, and attacked our stove top — squirting in so much cleaning fluid that the thing wouldn't work for three months. Many women of her generation have a cleaning fetish, but not many have actually cleaned one of their son's appliances to death.

My mother also believes that I'm obscenely overweight and possibly close to death. She will arrive wearing a solicitous look, pulling her white gloves on ever-tighter, as her eyes swivel between my belly and the stained kitchen benchtops. She will exercise self-control and decide to say nothing — the corners of her pursed lips twitching with the effort. It is an effort at self-control that will break down in a spectacular fashion sometime on the second day.

And so I scrub and I diet.

I say to Jocasta: 'Why should you be responsible for the fact that I'm just the tiniest bit overweight? It's nothing to do with you. I don't care what she says, and neither should you.'

Jocasta replies in a dull, beaten-down monotone, as she scrubs at a recalcitrant piece of skirting: 'You know nothing,' she says. 'It's the patriarchy. The woman always gets the blame. The mother blames the wife, and never the precious son. Oh, no. He's *perfect*.'

It's true my mother has two photographs of me on her hall table. They are side by side — one of me at age fourteen, looking painfully thin. And another, taken a year ago, in which I'm photographed from below in a way that makes me look like Marlon Brando after a binge. Says Jocasta: 'It's her way of saying, "This is him when I looked after him; and here he is under the regime of that fat girlfriend of his."'

Jocasta squirts some Spray n'Wipe onto her cloth and starts singing a mournful slave song from the American south. She appears hopeful that some sort of chariot might swing low and take her to heaven, sometime before Wednesday.

Says Jocasta: 'She'll think the shower recess is dirty, but actually it isn't. The tiles are permanently stained, and so is the grouting, but I'll get the blame. I think you should regrout it.'

I reply: 'I'm not going to regrout the whole bathroom just so my mother can have a single shower on Christmas Day. You're insane.'

I clean the ceiling of the kitchen with sugar soap — a job which sends rivulets of caustic chemicals straight into my eyes. After further discussion with Jocasta, I then decide to regrout the bathroom. The process takes about four hours. The house is getting cleaner and surely — by mere dint of sweaty effort — I'm getting thinner. Maybe this time we'll reach Day Three of The Visit before my mother and I have our standard conversation:

HER: 'I can see you're not doing anything about your weight problem.'
ME: 'It's nothing to do with you, Mum. I'm not that fat and, besides, why don't you mind your own business?'
HER: 'I would, but it's a health issue, darling.'

For her, it's like trying to ignore the huge elephant in the room, the one named Richard. For me, it's a matter of contemplating my time in Long Bay should I snap and kill her. So I exercise as I clean — wiping the cupboards, polishing the benchtops and chucking expired medicines from the bathroom cabinet.

Jocasta says: 'Don't leave any medicine bottles at all. They are evidence of illness. She'll think we got sick because we live like pigs in our own filth.' Jocasta is on her hands and knees in the bathtub, scrubbing while she sings 'Oh Lord, Will You Let My People Go' in a yearning alto.

I wash down the back of the house, vacuum some crumbs out of the kitchen drawers and wash down the kitchen windows. As I peer through the soap scum into the kitchen, I see Jocasta collecting up the cleaning products, putting them in boxes and hiding them in cupboards, so that my mother cannot once again kill our stove. After years of preparing for my father's visits by removing all the alcohol, she now repeats the procedure. Instead of hiding the Scotch, this time she hides all the bottles of Domestos.

Meanwhile, I tackle our bedroom — discovering five apple cores beneath my desk and a beer bottle under the bed. The thought strikes: maybe my mother is right and we do live like pigs in our own filth.

Outside the back door, Jocasta is spraying the dog with air-freshener and singing 'Death Be My Friend and Take Me to My Lord', while I consult her list. Three days to go and all I have to do is clean the car, scrub the steps and lose six kilos.

The day before Christmas, my mother arrives. She looks at the house but says nothing. She then gives Jocasta a hug, after which she draws me aside, saying Jocasta is 'a natural mother'. This, I'm pretty sure, is my mother's codeword for 'fat'. At least she hasn't said anything about me. We go for a walk, me slightly ahead with the dog, while Jocasta walks along with my mother. I take comfort from the fact that (a) I'm not that overweight — not after all that cleaning; and (b) to the extent that I am a little overweight, Jocasta will get all the blame.

I can feel my mother's eyes on me as I walk. I sense she is battling with herself about whether to say anything. As usual, it is a battle her better self rapidly loses. 'Ah,' sighs my mother, confiding in Jocasta. 'It's such a shame. He used to be taller.'

Desperate Husbands

For us guys, it's great to have a new drama show to hook into — one that's about our lives. This time around it's the new hit series *Desperate Husbands*. It's only been on for one season but already you hear of groups of guys getting together — maybe one brings the beers, another the nachos — and settling down to watch. There's been so much TV for women recently — *Sex and the City* and *Footballers' Wives* — we guys are hungry for the chance to get together, relax, and reserve a little time for ourselves, and for our friendship. This new show — *Desperate Husbands* — gives us that chance.

All of us have our favourite characters. For me, it's Bryn, the super-husband, whose hair is always perfect, whose lawn is always mowed and whose edges are always perfectly trimmed. He's got the gym-toned body, pulls a good salary, and can turn out a plate of fluffy muffins. Yet his wife doesn't appreciate him. I guess I perceive something of myself in his situation.

Other guys in our group connect with different characters. They come around Monday night to sit and watch, to laugh and cry. 'That could be me,' says my friend Tim, as he watches one of the Desperate Husbands wade into the swimming pool, in a full business suit, in order to untangle a kink in his Kreepy Krauly automatic pool cleaner. 'I think some people just don't realise the pressure we guys are under, trying to balance everything — the job, the kids, the pool chemicals. Finally you snap. Before you know it, there are chlorine stains all over your best Armani.'

Maybe that's why we all appreciate the 'wish-fulfilment' character — the middle-aged man who's having a steamy affair with his eighteen-year-old housemaid. How we laughed when the wife came home from the office and demanded to know what the housemaid had been doing all day! We knew exactly what she'd been doing: having glorious sex with our Desperate Husband while we cheered them on! We especially loved the scene later on — where the middle-aged bloke has to get up in the middle of the night and secretly iron a whole basketful of pleated dresses — all to convince his wife that the housemaid had done some *real* work during the day.

'Been there, done that!' we all shouted as we watched, wolfing down the nachos — even though the truth is we wouldn't dare. All of us know too well the difficulties involved in ironing pleats.

Why do we guys like the show so much? I guess it's because we feel locked in a little; we feel our lives are on a railway track, all laid out. It's great to imagine that we could jump the tracks every now and then — and do something really *desperate*. After the show is finished, we sit there, polishing off the last of the nachos, draining the last of the beers, and we start to dream. Could we really just throw off the ropes? The mortgages? The soccer-practice chauffeur service? The emasculated deference to the boss at work? Could there be another way to start each day, other than with ironing a shirt for work?

Who knows? But with the help of *Desperate Husbands* we're starting to open up a little; confessing the ways in which middle age is hitting us. Sitting around after the show, we admit we used to think about sex all the time . . . but now it's different. 'I don't know what's gone wrong,' says my mate Ryan, staring pensively at the last of the nachos. 'Sometimes these days I can go a whole minute without thinking about sex.' The rest of us nod supportively, trying not to let the shock show on our faces. *A whole minute without thinking about sex.* Ryan's situation is worse than we thought.

Desperate Husbands is certainly having its effect. Just yesterday, Tim found he was no longer wearing a tie to work; he's also swapped his cotton shirts for a no-iron drip-dry number. 'I just felt: why not? It's time to take some risks.'

Ryan, meanwhile, is now considering having an affair — just as soon as he clears his credit card sufficiently to be able to pay for the motel room. He also wants to get a bit further ahead in his yoga so he doesn't do in his back during whatever athletic sex session might be ahead. But after that: straight into an affair, as steamy as he can get it.

And me? Well, I'm just going to stop trying so hard. Sure, I'll keep the body perfect; and continue to use sufficient hair-product so that I always look my best. But this weekend, I may well drop the kids off at the wrong end of the oval for their game; and then let the grass verge go without its weekly trim. After that: an affair, or perhaps skydiving.

Once husbands get desperate, you never know what chaos will ensue.

devoted

She looks worried but
I'm not too concerned.
The children are alive. The
house has not burnt down.
There have been no major
outbreaks of disease.
Frankly, I think I deserve
a bloody medal.

In Germany, just don't mention the door

We're in Kmart, the four of us. We refuse to let our anxiety show, even though Batboy is about to get on the plane. He'll be gone for two and a half months: overseas, on student exchange. Apart from a week at school camp, it's his first time away. His younger brother thinks it's funny, as he watches us pick through the store buying final supplies. 'Our little boy is all grown up,' says The Space Cadet, using a faux-American accent. 'Oh, I'm so proud.' We all ignore him. This is no time for joking.

'What you really need,' Jocasta tells Batboy, 'is a Chapstick. You can put it on your lips so they don't crack with the cold.'

Batboy says he doesn't need a Chapstick but Jocasta seems very focused on the idea. 'I *really* think you need a Chapstick,' she insists, her voice edged with what can only be described as hysteria. But Batboy is adamant, and the two of them pause, locked in a stand-off somewhere between Toiletries and Cosmetics.

'They are really good,' says Jocasta, picking one up from the display. 'They really protect you.' She hits the word 'protect' a little hard and holds the Chapstick upright in her hand as if it's a miniature wand from *The Lord of the Rings*. She looks as if she may suffer a grand mal seizure unless she somehow manages to get the Chapstick into Batboy's backpack.

'I really don't need the Chapstick,' replies Batboy, amiably enough.

'Now come along,' says The Space Cadet, dancing in between them and using the same faux-American accent. 'Let's not have a fight just before our little boy goes.'

The Space Cadet thinks he's enormously funny. I think he may be right.

'Well okay,' says Jocasta finally. 'You can always buy one overseas, once you're there.'

I can see her line of thought: the boy is about to handle ten weeks in a rural village, bang in the middle of rural Germany. It will be winter, his host family doesn't speak English and a bus passes only once a day. Given all this, lip care may be the least of his worries.

Not that the family doesn't sound wonderful — even if they do live a very isolated, traditional life, quite different from anything Batboy has experienced before. His host brother has been emailing him every day, describing the farm, the motorbikes and the animals. Only a few days back he emailed very excitedly: 'Good news, visiting brother! Father says we will hold off the slaughtering of the cow until the day you arrive.'

Batboy took the news surprisingly well. I guess there's no cure for jetlag like a few hours of playful cow butchering. Already he has been told about how they have their own pigs, from which they make their own sausages, and chickens which they slaughter for Sunday lunch. Either he'll come home twice the size and wearing *Lederhosen*; or as a rake-thin vegetarian.

Certainly he'll come back Lutheran. When we first received details of his host family, we sneakily put them into Google, together with the name of the nearest village. What came up was a village diary, showing that their house was used every Tuesday for meetings of a local choir. According to our best effort at translation, the family comprises the principal members of the local Evangelical Lutheran Trombone Choir. A picture does form of Christmas Day: Batboy and his host brother working their way through a couple of family pigs, starting at the head and moving down, their *Lederhosen* tightening as their stomachs expand, while the rest of the family pump away on a trombone rendition of 'Silent Night'.

I'm momentarily concerned, but they send us a photo and everyone looks reassuringly normal. A friend tells me to ignore the word 'evangelical' — it just means they are normal Lutherans and not the sort of insane, wild-eyed Protestants you find in certain exotic out-of-the-way places. For instance: Sydney. He is, however, unable to explain neither the religious nor musical point of a choir consisting solely of massed trombones.

Back home, it's a few hours before departure and Batboy is packing the last of his things. A CD of Australian rock music, an old hardback copy of the poems of C.J. Dennis, two jars of Vegemite and his own body weight in Tim Tams. I go off to work and imagine him taking off. I keep looking at my watch and charting his progress. Above Brisbane now. Cairns. Singapore.

We have dinner, the remaining three of us. There's not many pots and plates to wash up and I remark on this fact to The Space Cadet, who's standing beside me as I scrub away, flicking my legs with his tea towel. 'You know why?' he says, with all the sensitivity of a younger brother. 'It's because that lard-arse isn't here.' I glance towards Jocasta, sitting on the couch with a faraway look. I guess she's also charting Batboy's progress — a dotted line arching through her mind, stretching from his bedroom to this new world of slaughtered cows, joyful trombones and home-made sausage.

We hosted an exchange student ourselves, only a few months before. Maria from northern Germany survived our odd family, so surely Batboy would survive his hosts. While Batboy is in the air, I find myself thinking about the time Maria spent with us. I always feel sorry for tourists who fall into our hands: we are so insistently proud of the town. Every spare minute Maria was here, we showed her the wonders of Sydney. 'Look at the Opera House. Isn't it the most beautiful building in the world? We're not leaving this spot until you agree with us that it is. I mean, how would you rate it, exactly, against the best buildings in, say, Europe?'

It's that wonderful mix of pride, bluster and deep insecurity that says so eloquently 'Australian'.

We certainly sent Maria back home with a very fine and detailed knowledge of Australia. Not only of the Opera

House. But of the flora and fauna as well. 'Isn't that koala amazing?' I say to her, as we walk through the animal park. 'And, quick, look at the wombats — how cute are they? The platypus, you know, is one of only two monotremes. And the Tasmanian devil is facing an amazing and terrifying epidemic of disease within Tasmania.'

With an exchange student to educate, I've suddenly turned into an effete version of the Crocodile Hunter. Everything is amazing, fantastic and incredible. Half-understood facts from school come tumbling out. Australia had a gold rush in the 1850s, I tell her. The gum is a sort of eucalypt. The wombat has a backward-facing pouch so that dirt doesn't fall in while it is digging.

I haven't had a chance to expound this stuff since Year 5 and I seize the opportunity with enthusiasm. Suddenly, I'm the Professor of All Knowledge; each barely remembered fact a jewel to place before the visitor. The merino is Australia's leading sheep. Pineapples are grown in Queensland. Australia has a bicameral system of government. I can't quite remember what a bicameral system of government is but it seems unlikely she'll ask. By this time we're driving home, and in the back seat of the car, Maria appears to have fallen into deep, deep slumber.

We pull up outside our place and Jocasta tries to awaken the visitor. 'Australia has nine of the ten most deadly snakes in the world,' Jocasta insists, as she tries to shake her awake. 'There are six states and two territories. And the water in the plughole goes the other way around.'

Maria is unfailingly polite. 'Really?' she says, squeezing her eyes open and shut to dislodge the sleep. 'How fascinating.'

'Oh, yes,' I say, 'and Burke and Wills got lost near a tree. Plus, the Hume Highway is named after an explorer called Hume, who grew up in a hovel. And Tasmania was circumnavigated by a man called Flinders, who was accompanied by a cat. The cat, of course, was later used to punish convicts in a way still not understood by historians.'

Says Maria: 'And, please, why does the water go the other way?'

'Ah well,' I answer, as we walk towards the door, 'that would be because . . . '

'Because,' Jocasta says, coming to my rescue, 'because of the way Australia is . . . '

'On the bottom of the world,' I take over. 'So there's more gravity, because of all the weight.'

Maria glances at us for a second and then thanks us. Her look says: 'I'm stuck here, 20,000 kilometres from home, living with mad people.'

We show her the rugby league on the television and make her Vegemite toast, which she describes as 'most interesting'. I show her a wattle tree and point out the bright yellow flowers. 'Fascinating, isn't it,' I say, 'that this, too, is a eucalypt?'

'Actually,' says Jocasta, 'it's an acacia.'

'Well, that's right,' I say. 'An acacia, thought to date from the time of dinosaurs. Older than anything you'd find in Europe.'

I decide I should give her a break from the learning — just as soon as I've taught her a little geology. Having once read the back of a Tim Flannery book, I feel pretty well equipped and so, as we help her into the house, I explain that Australia is the oldest land on the planet, possibly older than the planet itself, I can't be quite sure, but certainly older than Germany.

'Everything's been worn down over time. Imagine something just wearing you down, hour after hour, day after day.'

'Yes,' replies Maria, limping up the stairs, 'I can see how that might work.'

Will Batboy's host parents be like this: forcing him to express joy in every detail of German flora, fauna and geology? The days go past. He rings home after about a week. I say to him: 'I bet we overdid it when we imagined them living this really rural existence. You know, the trombone choir and the pig slaughtering. Now you've met them, I bet it's not like that at all.'

'In fact,' he says over the phone, 'it's more extreme than I imagined; more remote, more traditional.' He explains how his family never buys soft drink: the main drink is apple juice, crushed from their own orchard. They grow all their own food, right down to their own wheat, barley and spelt, an ancient grain which the mother grinds into flour. Only last night they had pizza with the base made from hand-ground spelt. For entertainment they really do have the church trombone choir, of which all the family are members. The only thing we didn't understand is that a trombone choir, for some reason, has more than just trombones. It has a variety of brass instruments. The whole village, he says, is heavy with brass instruments.

And yet, says Batboy, he's having fun. And he really admires his host father, Volker, and the rest of the family.

Ten weeks later he arrives back home. We greet him at the airport, thrilled to have him back. He has vastly improved German. In fact, his problem now is his English. 'My father, Volker, sent me out to collect some, some, you know, *Sägemehl*,' he says to us, the English word entirely lost to him. He acts out a sawing motion. 'You know, the white stuff that comes out of the tree.'

'Sawdust,' suggests Jocasta.

'That's it,' says Batboy, before running ahead with his sentence only to get tangled up once more, this time in a chainsaw. 'My father, Volker, cut the tree down with a, you know, a *Kettensäge*.'

But it's this 'my father' stuff that gets me. I know the exchange student is supposed to embrace the new family, but does Batboy have to be quite so enthusiastic? As the days go on, it's all Volker this and Volker that. Maria was never like this about me, despite all the effort I put into her education.

We stand at the back door, looking out at our small suburban backyard. 'On our farm,' says Batboy, 'we have an orchard. And our own small plantation of pines to supply the family with timber. And, of course, our own cows and pigs. Volker oversees it all.'

Why do I suddenly feel so inadequate, looking out over our suburban block, and wondering how to meet my son's newly expanded expectations. Perhaps we could slip a small piggery into the space between the fence and the clothesline, but I'm buggered where I can put the pine plantation.

'If my father needs a door, he'll just make one out of timber instead of buying it at the shop,' says Batboy, trying to explain how it's done, before giving in to my insistent interruptions. 'I know, I know,' I say, somewhat petulantly. 'You don't need to tell me. I've done it myself. Look at the door on the shed. Built by me. Out of timber. Volker's not the only father who knows how to build a door.'

'Ah yes,' says Batboy. 'But Volker's timber comes from the plantation not the timber yard. And what about the hinges? I suppose you bought yours at the shop? When my father builds a door we search the farm for scrap metal, melt it down in a furnace and then cast our own hinges. They've been doing it this way for centuries.'

I'm fast losing patience with Volker and his thrifty German ways. I fight off an urge to mention the war.

With the combination of farm work and healthy food, Batboy has lost six kilos and put on a layer of muscle, all in ten weeks. And this despite the cakes. 'My mother makes a couple of cakes every day,' he brightly tells Jocasta, as she stands, weary from work, stirring that night's bolognaise. 'She makes chocolate cake, caramel cake and a cake called The Waves of the Danube, which has chocolate on top, forming these tiny little waves. It's delicious.'

'I bet it is,' says Jocasta bleakly. She rolls her eyes and whispers to me so that Batboy can't hear. She's only been home from work for half an hour and considers it 'a bloody miracle' that any food at all is being provided, never mind a cake in the shape of little waves. Besides, it's not as if she wasn't planning to provide some dessert for the boy. Already a box of No Frills brand chocolate paddle pops lies waiting in our freezer.

'For dinner,' Batboy continues, unaware of the growing threat to his life, 'we would have meat from our own animals. My mother would make it into these beautiful stews.' He then starts describing the process of slaughtering pigs, collecting the blood for blood sausage, and removing the organs; at which point I take over the stirring of the bolognaise as Jocasta, turning green, retires defeated from the kitchen.

Of course, as each day goes past, Farmboy starts to convert back into Batboy. He stops using German words quite so often; and stops getting hungry at about five — his body clock no longer on the lookout for a slice or two of The Waves of the Danube. When he uses the word 'our', it increasingly refers to this rectangle of Sydney suburbia; 'my father' is increasingly his hinge-buying, supermarket-shopping Australian father; and 'my mother' his overstretched, non-cake-baking Australian mother.

He sprawls in front of the TV, an apple in his hand, and warily contemplates a small bottle of Coke. Some day soon he will be pleased to be home, but right now he still has the tastes of a rural German traditionalist — and a ruddy, frostbitten complexion to match.

Jocasta shakes her head. If only she'd insisted on that Chapstick.

Home alone

A couple of decades ago, when Jocasta would go interstate for work, the result was a big upswing in my standard of living. When the neighbourhood women discovered she was away, they would bring me food. Spanakopita, Monday. A nice Italian casserole on Tuesday. Portuguese Cozido on Wednesday. Jocasta's now been in Melbourne for two weeks and nary a casserole has appeared. I've sent The Space Cadet out onto the pavement looking hungry, without so much as a flying kebab in response.

These days, you are meant to cope. In fact, I'm not even allowed to mention that it's been a bit of a challenge.

'Melbourne? Lovely. Two weeks? Super. I'll hardly notice you've gone.' This, I think, goes for both men and women. Since housework and childcare is such a contested area, you can never admit the crucial nature of your partner's contribution. 'Getting the children to sport on time? Oh, that was no trouble at all. And isn't it pleasant having that hour walking around the park in the bracing air while you wait for them to finish?'

Normally, I do the washing and ironing during the week and she does the weekday cooking. That way we've got plenty of time on the weekends to have a stand-up row about the cleaning. Now I have to do all three plus argue with myself about the state of the kitchen. Lord knows how single parents cope.

By Tuesday, the kitchen floor already features eight dead cockroaches plus a patina of dropped food. By Thursday, there are fifteen dead cockroaches, who appear to have organised their bodies across the floor to spell out the phrase 'Sweep Me'.

The parenting quandaries soon multiply. First problem: the phrase 'Mum would have let me'. Even when we are *both* in the house, The Space Cadet knows how to play one against the other. Better, if the other is 800 kilometres away. And so he makes the claim that, after soccer practice, Jocasta showers him with junk food. This seems unlikely. I deny the request and instead offer a drink of water. The Space Cadet says I'm being 'harsh' — so falling in love with the word that he starts calling me 'Mr Harsh' and 'Inspector Harsh' and 'Professor Harsh' and 'AA Harsh' and 'Mrs Harsh'. It's a joke that lasts all fortnight. My new name, in some creative variant, greets my every parenting decision.

And if The Space Cadet thinks I'm harsh, Batboy believes I'm incompetent — blaming every household problem on the fact that I'm running the show. Bringing us to the rule: the further away the other parent is, the more wonderful they become.

For the last couple of months Batboy has been learning to referee soccer games in the belief that he'll earn twice what they pay at Kmart. Already he's been issued with his official red and yellow cards. 'You're gone, mate, gone,' he says producing the yellow card with a flourish. 'Mum's been away for four days, and look — there's no bread and there's no milk.' He seems delighted with this observation. I offer him cereal with a splash of water and mumble that things aren't so bad. Batboy stares me down. 'Are you telling me I'm wrong? That's breach Y16. Dissent against the ref by word or deed. That's a red carder.' I take a silent vow. I will find the person who thought it was a good idea to give a high-school student a sense of power. Then I'll kill him.

Jocasta, I notice, dropped large amounts of laundry into the basket just before her departure. She also did 'a clean-out' of the fridge — throwing out any food past its use-by date. This, of course, is precisely the sort of food that can sustain a family through a crisis. I conclude she has a hidden plan to make the house fall apart during my stewardship, thus proving her contention that she does all the housework and I do nothing. I resolve to defeat her.

By Friday, my head is pounding due to the constant alcohol abuse. Batboy notes that his soccer referee's uniform is still in the wash, which is 'conduct warranting a caution'. He waves a yellow card in my direction. There are now twenty-two dead cockroaches, their bodies arranged to spell out the phrase 'He's Losing It'. This is when Jocasta rings in, wondering how we're all getting on. Before answering, I remind myself: if you admit you're not coping, it's just another way of confessing that she normally does more than her share of this stuff. 'Fine,' I say. 'Absolute breeze. Getting a lot of reading in, actually. Great to be able to cook every night. A real pleasure.'

The only problem with this barefaced lie is the chaos that surrounds me. The phone call ends and I set to work. In the days ahead, the illusion must be created that we coped effortlessly. I square my shoulders and order the children into action. I am Major-General Harsh and we shall have the house spotless. I start scrubbing at various surfaces and — to save time — cook all the family's meals in one go: an army-sized quantity of bolognaise sauce, sufficient to last ten consecutive meals.

I tackle the ironing and by the second Wednesday every basket is empty, even the Too Hard Basket — the one full of the pleats and weird pockets. The kitchen, though, appears to be fighting back against my attempts to clean it. Spaghetti sauce is evident on most surfaces, and fifty-seven deceased cockroaches now litter the floor, their bodies spelling out 'She's Winning'.

By Monday, Batboy is growing suspicious. Spooning down his spaghetti bolognaise for the eighth successive night, an idea forms: 'We've had this meal before, haven't we?'

'Maybe once or twice,' I reply. Batboy says he feels sick. Weakly he slips his red card out of his pocket. 'Repeated abuse of a ref,' he says, his voice trembling.

Back in the kitchen, the cockroaches have reorganised themselves into a giant clock-face, counting down the minutes until Jocasta's return. With the cockroach clock ticking, I work through the night, scrubbing and cleaning. I remove all signs of the town of Bologna and its famous sauce. I sweep up the cockroaches. I buy milk and bread. Panting slightly, I arrive home with seconds to spare.

'The place looks great,' says Jocasta, walking in.

'Oh, does it?' I say, glancing up from the newspaper. 'I hadn't noticed.'

The scene is perfect save for Batboy, who is lying by the back door holding his stomach and groaning. Looking quite red in the face, he keeps mouthing the words 'the bolognaise'.

'Is he all right?' Jocasta asks.

'Oh, yeah,' I say. 'Just feigning injury. Taking a dive. It's offence Y35. He better watch it. He'll be up for a yellow card.'

She looks worried but I'm not too concerned. The children are alive. The house has not burnt down. There have been no major outbreaks of disease. Frankly, I think I deserve a bloody medal.

Twisted tongues

On holiday in Germany, I'd been standing in the queue of tourists outside the new Reichstag. Along with everyone else, I was becoming increasingly testy about the prim German *Madchen* in charge of the doors. She was allowing only a few people to wait in the spacious warmth of the foyer and seemed to be enjoying the power trip of watching the rest of us freeze in the snow. '*Ungefickt zum Dienst,*' muttered my German friend through chapped lips, and others nearby agreed. '*Ungefickt zum Dienst,*' they chorused. My friend translated: 'It means someone who's doing a boring job but also hasn't had sex recently, and is therefore taking it out on everybody else. You would say she is "unfucked for work".'

It's a fantastic concept and in the weeks that follow, it warms my heart to be able to understand the true cause of any bad and snarly service that I might receive. And yet, for the most part, in the battle between me and the German language, I am nearly always the loser. In the Munich cafe on the first night, I summoned the waitress and demonstrated my skill in speaking German. 'My wife will have the chicken, my younger son will have the sausages, and your son, I think, will have the schnitzel.' Perhaps she's used to tourists advising her what to feed her children. I don't know. She didn't say anything but looked a little grim. Now I come to think of it, I may also have demanded a large beer be immediately served to her husband.

Another problem. It's our first trip overseas for twelve years: my knowledge of all the languages has fallen apart, and so has the binding on our travel dictionaries. I discover a whole chunk of the German one is missing — everything from 'cheap' through to 'thing'. I can ask for directions to the art gallery or the zoo but not much else. A visit to the cinema would have been nice . . . but I see we've missed out by just one or two pages. And how strange to discover that all the very best food and drink lies somewhere in the middle of the alphabet. I know the kids want hot chocolate or Coke with their meal, but wouldn't apple juice do? Or maybe some tonic water? And what to eat? Their choice: anchovies, artichokes, veal or vension.

The dictionary probably fell apart on the plane while I made my last-minute revisions. Some other Qantas customer is, no doubt, travelling Germany right now armed with a chunk of my book, gleefully attending football matches, ordering cocktails, gulping down mugs of hot chocolate and asking directions to the mixed nude sauna. I hope he's having a good time, the bastard.

Disgruntled, I purchase a cheap German phrase book. This one is intact, but reflects a somewhat dodgy morality.

There's a whole section on dating, for instance — 'Are you free this evening?', 'Are you waiting for someone?' and 'Can we go back to your place now?'. It all seems a bit forward since, by very use of the book, you're admitting you can't understand a word she is saying. As you haltingly read these phrases from the book in the middle of the nightclub, will she really believe your main interest is her mind, her passion for medieval architecture and her views on global warming?

My language woes only deepen once we cross into Italy. On the train I try to memorise a list of simple phrases — 'Hello', 'Goodbye', 'How much is it?'. The trick is saying them in the right order. Arriving at the *pensione* the first evening, I stride in, shake the man's hand and greet him warmly in Italian: 'Well, goodbye,' I say to him. He looks somewhat confused. No doubt when we leave, I'll pay the bill, pick up the bags and shout, 'Well, hello,' as I stumble out the door.

Jocasta, inevitably, has the language down pat, and rushes into cake shops and orders this or that '*questa*'. It turns out this is the Italian for 'I'll have one of those', but I'm left with the impression it's the term for a particular gooey pastry. For some reason Jocasta finds it amusing when I inquire at the restaurant that night whether dessert might include any of those 'really beautiful *questos*'.

We move on, travelling through Slovenia on the way to France, which is like going to Melbourne on the way from Sydney to Brisbane. I buy a Slovenian guidebook, and we sit down to eat. Almost immediately I realise my guidebook doesn't include the phrase for ordering a beer. Incredulous, I flip through again and still find it missing, even from the section marked 'emergencies'. In fact, the only thing listed in the drinks section is the local pear liquor — Hruska.

Somewhat later I discover this is also the sound you make after you've drunk too much of it.

For some reason Paris seems easier. Despite my complete lack of French, I discover I'm able to translate an entire advertisement about the strip club next to our hotel. It's like a curious mystical ability: I'm a sex savant. I read the sign to Jocasta, freely translating as I go. The club features women who dance without their tops on and, later in the night, remove their trousers. Alcohol, I read aloud, is served to gentlemen at very reasonable prices. And the women are very beautiful. The place is called either The House of Pain or The House of Bread. Or possibly both. I can't be sure. It may be that they strip off then beat each other with bread sticks. Odd, certainly, but the French *are* odd. The point is, I am able to understand nearly every word.

Slovenia aside, it's the same with beer. Wherever we travel, I can order it immediately and in any quantity. I'm now convinced I could attend a strip club and get pissed anywhere in the world. Is this the collective unconscious of which Jung wrote? Are Australian men the only ones born with this remarkable linguistic gift?

We head home with a stopover in Los Angeles. My linguistic confusion grows all the more intense. I try to copy the American way of speaking English. It's 'real' good, not 'really'; 'five x', not 'five times'; and 'two-thousand-five' instead of 'two thousand *and* five'. They are so spectacularly busy they just don't have time for those extra syllables. Even the children are flat out, forced to call it 'math' and not 'maths'. They'd love to add that final 's' but, real sorry, just don't have the time. In a park, I even spot a sign advising a 'No Thru Road'. I imagine the poor park supervisor, up to his neck in work. 'I'm just not in a position to muck around with letters that really aren't pulling their weight.'

Of course, once I get home, I realise that it's the Australian language which is the strangest of all. We're a nation of underestimators. It's the only place in the world where an atrocious act is described as 'a bit ordinary', while an act of genius is 'not half bad'. The first day of spring, in which birds are trilling, the air throbs with heat and scent, and the sky is a brilliant azure blue, is described as 'not too bad at all'.

It must be tough for American visitors, given that their usage is a little more upbeat. Ask an American 'How are you?' and it's seen as a cue to deliver some advertising copy: 'You know what? I'm terrific. I'm awesome. I'm fantastic.' The person saying this is often slipping in and out of a coma, or lying in the gutter having been bankrupted for the fourteenth time.

This is not a problem for their fellow Americans. They simply employ the National Linguistic Deflator to the sentence, dividing all positive sentiments by 230 per cent, multiplying all negative notions by the power of ten, thus concluding that the person is 'as good as can be expected, considering'.

In Australia, it's the opposite. The National Linguistic Inflator must be employed. Consider the following exchange:

'How are you?'

'Not bad. And you?'

'Can't complain.'

As is exceedingly obvious, the first person has just, minutes ago, won the Nobel Prize for Literature for his first experimental novel, while his friend has just made it into *Who Weekly*'s Most Sexy Person Alive double issue, despite his work as a brain surgeon.

Of course, every community has its braggers and blowhards, but a true Australian discussion is like a perpetual round of misère, with the aim of losing every trick.

'Your car's looking good.'

'Come off it, it's full of dents and rust.'

'I've got to sell mine, it's so lousy.'

'At least you're free to sell. I still owe too much.'

'Gee, were you able to get a loan? They turned me down.'

Kerry Packer, billionaire, has 'a few bob'. Don Bradman, the world's greatest cricketer, was 'no slouch with the bat'. Meanwhile, someone truly incompetent is merely 'a bit average'. In fact, Australia is the only country in which a really evil person is called 'a *bit* of a bastard', while your best friend is 'a *total* bastard'.

At least we've got somewhere to go, linguistically speaking. In America, it's as if they've given a score of ten out of ten to the first player in the competition. If you are awesome and fantastic while slipping in and out of the coma, what do you say on a really good day? 'Actually, I've just won the Nobel Prize for Literature and been chosen as one of *Who Weekly*'s Most Sexy People in the Universe. So I guess I feel even *more* awesome than I did when I was falling in and out of that coma back there.'

This may be why younger Americans have fallen right off the scale of exaggeration and had to circle around to start again on the other side. Something really good is now 'sick' or 'wicked'. These words have been picked up by Australian teenagers, causing intergenerational bafflement, particularly once the attempt is made to translate it all back into Australian.

'The film was really sick, Dad.'

'It was sick? So, really bad, huh? So bad it was, like, a bit ordinary?'

'No it wasn't that bad. It was good. Really good.'

'How good? So good it wasn't that bad?'

'Aw, no, probably not *that* good.'

If Australians had landed on the moon, the speech would have gone, 'This is two small steps for man and a half-decent effort for mankind.' Everyone would then apply the National Linguistic Inflator to the speech, multiply everything by 173 per cent and work out the bloke was actually saying the whole thing was awesome.

It's then the country would stand to attention and shout as one towards the moon: 'Mate, no one likes a bignoter,' at which point the Aussie astronaut would stomp off and sulk, and we'd be forced to look to another language for an explanation.

Who knows? Maybe he was just a little *Ungefickt zum Dienst*.

I'm a little teapot

We've had the same metal teapot for fifteen years, but recently it has become too battered to use. I set out to buy another, searching the net for a retailer who stocks our brand. This is how I discover our model was recalled, back in 1995. Apparently, it leaks lead poison into the tea, in a way proved to cause intellectual impairment among laboratory rats.

I break the news to Jocasta and she is not happy. 'I don't know why you bought a metal teapot in the first place. Didn't you realise there might be lead in it? Your son will now almost certainly fail his final exams and it will be all your fault.'

She suggests I go and sit on the naughty chair as payment for my crimes. Jocasta has been watching the TV show *Supernanny* and wants to try out some of the tips. According to the Supernanny, offenders should be sentenced to the naughty chair for a period of minutes equal to their age in years — five minutes if you are five years old, six minutes if you are six.

This is fine advice, except when the miscreant is, like me, forty-six. I tell Jocasta I think three-quarters of an hour is too long, but she is adamant.

I spend some time on the naughty chair contemplating my crime. I realise I feel quite upbeat. Everyone else in society has an excuse for their failings — excuses such as poverty, racial intolerance and ingrained prejudice towards the left-handed. Finally I have mine. Oh, bliss. I've been poisoned by my teapot. Suddenly, it's clear — the bad temper, the over-reliance on alcohol, the oversensitivity to criticism — it's all the fault of the teapot.

Jocasta sits at the kitchen table, glumly dunking a teabag. 'You're like the Dr Crippen of the inner west,' she says.

I decide to award myself remission of sentence for good behaviour. I arise from the naughty chair, pour a glass of wine to celebrate my release and sink into the couch. By now, Jocasta has told the children about the teapot and Batboy has decided he may as well stop studying for his end-of-school exams. 'I'd wondered why I couldn't understand a word of Shakespeare,' he says resignedly, turning his attention to the TV. 'And why those Russian names in World War II were so hard to remember. If it wasn't for that teapot, I wouldn't be in this situation. The whole thing is hopeless.'

He busies himself drinking water in an effort, he says, 'to leach the lead out of my system'.

I try to work out just how much lead we've ingested and, therefore, how much the teapot is to blame for our various shortcomings. I do the numbers — as best I can considering I'm a man suffering severe mental damage. Three cups a day, for twenty years, with two extra cups on both Saturday and Sunday, comes to a grand total of, give me a minute . . . well, a lot. If I had not been systemically poisoned by my own teapot I may be able to offer a firmer figure.

I have a better idea: I will work backwards from all the disappointments I've suffered. It's probably the most accurate way to get a good fix on just how much lead I've consumed. Why, for example, have my books never sold as well as those of Dan Brown and J.K. Rowling? Why am I unable to win a single game of squash, even if I hand-pick the most asthmatic, lard-arsed of opponents?

And why am I yet to win a significant literary prize? Or, for that matter, a prize for medicine, science or peace?

That teapot has a lot to answer for.

Once in a mood like this, you start to go through your whole life, blow by disastrous body blow. I remember when I first left school, I tried to get a job at the bottom rung of the television industry. My idea was to start as a coffee boy and then rise to become the director of TV soap operas. The coffee boy job, however, eluded me. I had aimed low, and missed.

Fair enough, this happened *before* I bought the teapot; I have to accept that the teapot may not be to blame for *all* life's disappointments. But if not the teapot, it must be something else. There are those aluminium frypans we used to use, and which are still stuck up the back of the cupboard. The fibro garage we had at home when I was growing up. The flightpath overhead. The fluoride in the water supply . . .

I wonder about the laboratory rats — the source of the original case against the teapot. How, exactly, do they test these things? How good is the evidence? I imagine the rats sitting in their cages with a tiny miniature tea service. 'Milk?' asks one rat of the other, its little pinkie held aloft as it pours. 'Yes,' says his companion rat, 'and a couple of sugars, if you don't mind.'

I idly open a beer, wondering how they test the level of intellectual impairment in tea-drinking rats. Perhaps they screen repeated episodes of *Supernanny* and see how long it takes to drive them insane with boredom.

Batboy is still staring at the TV in a glum sort of way. 'I just knew there was some reason I found it so hard to settle down and study. Mum's right. I don't why you'd buy such a thing. I'm almost certain to fail however hard I study.'

At this point he is struck by an idea, and his mood suddenly lifts. 'Perhaps I could apply for some sort of special dispensation.'

For somebody poisoned by his parents' teapot, the boy is not as stupid as you might think. He's onto something. Perhaps we should all apply for some sort of special dispensation. Surely you, too, have some sort of excuse.

Title fight

'We should watch *Dad's Army*,' I say, holding up the DVD I bought three months ago. 'It's crap,' chorus Batboy and The Space Cadet, using the English language with all their usual skill and precision. I know they love the *Blackadder* series, so I try a fresh tack. 'Ben Elton, who wrote *Blackadder*, says that *Dad's Army* is great,' I tell them. 'I once heard him say that it was his favourite comedy ever.'

'You said that last time you tried to make us watch it,' says The Space Cadet, shaking his head. He turns to his mother: 'Dad's now on some sort of endless loop.'

Owning a small collection of DVDs is a wonderful thing, but it creates new conflicts. Before DVD, you'd all agree to watch television and confront a choice of five shows. Two would be too violent, one would be an Albanian dog-poisoning movie on SBS, and the other would be hosted by

Eddie McGuire. Result: you watch the creaky pommy drama on the ABC and no one's in a position to complain.

Now there's the shelf of DVDs and videos: thirty choices, all the time. But here's the problem: buy a new DVD movie, and Batboy and his brother will watch it twenty-four times in the first three days. Later, having owned the thing for three months, I suggest I might like to watch the movie for a second time and they stare at me in mute disbelief. By now, they've watched it 137 times, know the whole script by heart and are arguing over the dolly track placement in scenes ten through to fifteen.

They've even tried to inject some interest by watching it with the Polish subtitles, so often they could probably now order coffee for two in a Gdansk shipyard cafe. Worse, they behave as if somehow the movies are going to breed, right there on the DVD shelf, and that new choices will suddenly appear. Why else do they keep scanning the row 'just to see if there's something really good'?

I try to talk sense into them: 'There's nothing we haven't watched a million times. The only thing left is *Dad's Army*.'

'It's crap.'

'Well, Ben Elton says . . .'

And so it's back to scanning the shelves. And here's the other problem with the DVD. A person — say, for instance, me — makes a single purchasing error and it just sits there, ready to draw comment during every scan of the DVD shelf.

'Ah, great,' says The Space Cadet, with a level of sarcasm only possible if you are a thirteen-year-old boy. 'Here's Woody Allen's *Curse of the Jade Scorpion*. We could watch that. Or we could hit ourselves over the head with a chair, which might be more fun. Good one, Dad.'

'Yeah,' agrees Batboy. 'Good one, Dad'.

They say exactly these words, in exactly this tone of voice, every time they look through the shelf and come across *The Curse of the Jade Scorpion*, which, it must be admitted, *is* crap. I turn to Jocasta: 'I don't know what's wrong with these boys, they're now on some sort of endless loop.'

It's at this point we mount an expedition to the video shop, where a whole new world of misery and indecision awaits. It's a testament to Hollywood that you can have a choice of 300 new releases, made with a combined budget of $15.5 gazillion dollars, and still not find a single movie worth hiring. How they do it God only knows (although the continuing existence of Jerry Bruckheimer may be a factor worth considering).

Adding to our problems is my inability to remember which movies we've seen. I ring Jocasta. 'How about *Spy Games*?'

'We watched it . . . yesterday,' says Jocasta. 'OK, not yesterday. But last week. What's wrong with you?'

What's wrong with me is the way all Hollywood movie titles sound essentially the same. I scan the shelves: *Extreme Summer, Extreme Blow, Blow Hard, Blow Up, Blow Off, Pay Off, Back Off, Back Pay, Extreme Back Pain* . . .

The Space Cadet wants to hire a shoot-'em-up called *Summer Death Blow*; Batboy wants to hire some wintry epic about the siege of Stalingrad; and I fancy a morbid drama about life in a stifling small town. By some process that I still don't understand, we emerge with *Legally Blonde Two*.

We arrive home and I'm relieved to discover we didn't view it yesterday. 'It looks crap,' says Jocasta, using the language with all her usual skill and precision.

The movie is OK but leaves us hungry, still wanting more. The Space Cadet scans the shelves. He does his *Curse of the Jade Scorpion* speech. I go and fetch *Dad's Army* and do my Ben Elton speech. Jocasta puts her head in her hands and weeps. Since we got the DVD, I have the feeling this family is on some sort of endless loop.

Brew ha-ha

Batboy's latest hobby is home-brewed beer — an interest chosen for its capacity to chew up whole afternoons and thus prevent any study for his end-of-school exams. The idea first emerges on Saturday morning in an attempt to avoid an essay on World War II. Batboy is due to spend a whole day with Hitler in his bunker and is desperate to find a means of escape.

He wants me to accompany him to the home-brew shop and to fund the purchase of some gear. Or, as he puts it, 'invest in the equipment'. His speech is eloquent in terms of the scientific principles he might learn and the opportunity it will give him to understand production processes in what he calls this 'brand-name obsessed and pre-packaged society'.

I stand back impressed. People attack the Higher School Certificate, but it certainly equips students with a magnificent ability to bullshit their parents.

I am initially reluctant, however. I don't want to encourage drinking; I don't want to encourage time-wasting; and I don't want to deny Hitler a little company in his bunker. But Batboy assures me he will enjoy the merest sip of the brew. His main interest is his father, and the provision of a cheap, potable and regular supply of fluids.

There is a pause while we stare each other down. It is in this silence that he plays his masterstroke. 'It's tax-free alcohol, Dad.'

Jocasta has often criticised me for tardiness. There can be no such criticism this time. Within minutes of those intoxicating words being uttered — the term 'tax-free' coquettishly rubbing itself up alongside the word 'alcohol' — I find myself behind the wheel of the ute, motoring towards Gladesville.

Our 'investment' comes to $80, for which we are given a bewildering array of tubs and tubes. We decide we will make a lager-style beer, flavoured with Hersbrucker German hops. We are given an instruction sheet. Back home we set to work. We boil and we sterilise, we pour and we mix. We argue over the recipe. The Space Cadet decides to get involved. 'When it says fill to twenty-two litres, does that include the two litres you started with, or is it extra to that?' he asks, peering at the instructions. We're unsure, so we split the difference.

The Space Cadet encourages me to drink some packaged beer, 'because we really need the bottles'. Jocasta stands in the kitchen, arms folded, watching this scene unfold: a thirteen-year-old being enticed by his father into the world of alcoholism. From the look on her face, she's going to ring the child welfare people any minute and suggest an intervention.

Batboy, meanwhile, works on the computer, designing and printing the labels. He has located a photograph of himself in *Lederhosen*, drinking a beer, taken while on student exchange in Germany. He places it on the label beneath the brand name 'Papa Glover's German-style Lager'. Across the bottom he has added the slogan: 'The authentic taste you only get from Papa.' This amuses Jocasta sufficiently to buy us a little more time.

The plastic brewing tub has a thermometer stuck on the outside: one must place the tub so that it achieves a temperature of twenty to twenty-four degrees. Over the next two days I try it in various positions, including the laundry (too cold) and the living room (too hot). The only place it hits the right temperature is in The Space Cadet's bedroom, sitting on his desk. Sweeping aside his homework books and his collection of model planes, I plonk down the now bubbling and fermenting vat.

Jocasta looms at the doorway. 'You cannot turn your thirteen-year-old's bedroom into a brewery. Where's he going to do his homework? What about the smell of that thing? And what about the noise?'

It's true; the thing makes this incredibly loud sound. There's a water-filled valve in the top; the gas builds as the beer ferments and, at intervals of twenty or thirty seconds, it bubbles up like a loud, noxious fart, filling the air with a smell of rank hops. And yet the temperature is perfect.

I set up a bed for The Space Cadet in my room and volunteer to sleep in his bed beside the vat. I hardly sleep all night. Each time I start to nod off, I'm startled awake by another hugely loud, gurgling fart. In the morning, I stagger out to the kitchen. 'I hardly slept a wink,' I tell Jocasta, 'all night long next to this stinking, farting tub of booze.'

'Now you know how I feel most nights,' she replies, buttering toast.

Of course, the beer-brewing is only one of a number of activities designed by Batboy to make studying impossible.

His exam subjects appear to include English, history, German and a practical unit called procrastination. He is already showing an excellent grasp of the basic principles. Aside from brewing beer, he's playing squash, walking the dog and talking intensely to friends. He's suddenly got a thousand activities. He'll do anything as long as it's not studying.

He's not the only one. Our once-sleepy neighbourhood is ablaze with activity. The closer we get to the HSC, the more we are witnessing a cultural and sporting renaissance. One student has discovered a love of swimming — he walks to the pool, swims twenty laps, and then walks back home. He's fitter than he's ever been. If he takes the long way home, he can draw out the process to last most of the morning.

One girl, according to her mother, has discovered the joys of cleaning her own bedroom. So keen is she to avoid extension English, she's repacked all her clothes, wiped down all the shelves and vacuumed the blinds. After seventeen years of slovenly behaviour, she now has the neatest room in the house. A group of the boys, meanwhile, has formed a vegetable growing club, specialising in the competitive farming of chillies. No, really: chillies. When the aim is avoiding HSC study, no activity is too bizarre or too obscure.

Batboy has his beer brewing and his chilli farming, but there is still a risk that a few hours might be available for study, especially during the morning. That's why he's developed a sudden urge to read the *Sydney Morning Herald*. For years, I've tried to push him towards the newspaper, hoping he might develop an interest in current affairs. For years, he's rolled his eyes and mouthed the word 'boring'. Now, suddenly, under the gun of the HSC, he can't get enough of it. One morning this week, he read it for two hours straight — even enduring several pieces on Australian politics.

Maybe this is the real power of the HSC: it promises to create citizens of the future, and indeed it does — out of their very desperation to avoid the official curriculum. They'll do anything to get out of paying proper attention to HSC work, even becoming well-rounded, sociable citizens.

For the first time in living memory, they debate politics, play tennis and go jogging. No longer do they shrug and mumble when asked about their day. When their only alternative is study, they can think of nothing more delightful than leaning against the kitchen bench, chatting animatedly to their parents.

One seventeen-year-old boy last week offered to cook dinner for the family. An eighteen-year-old girl, meanwhile, offered to accompany her mother to the supermarket. The parents of both children are currently being treated for traumatic shock.

Yet even the most practised procrastinators will finally run out of excuses. Midway through this week, Batboy and friends discovered that this time had come. They had ridden the boundaries of their chilli farms, chatted endlessly to their parents, and tidied their bedrooms. Their beer brews were happily fermenting. Through some amazing coincidences, there was not a single eighteenth birthday party on that evening. They had read the *Herald*, even unto the arts pages. With a jolt of panic, they realised that ahead stretched two or three hours during which it was technically possible for them to study.

It was a nasty couple of minutes before one of the crew had the realisation: they had yet to organise their accommodation for schoolies week. Phew. Crisis averted. Organising schoolies week, if done properly, can take days — no, weeks. Which town to visit? Where to stay? And how to talk parents into handing over cash for a bond which has so little chance of ever being returned?

Batboy and his friends settled down to the task, while Jocasta nervously eyed the calendar.

'So this is the next few months,' she said, as the boys organised their trip. 'He procrastinates with his friends, you have the fun of helping him with the brewing beer, while I stare at the calendar, getting uptight on his behalf. And what happens at the end of this process? He gets to go off on schoolies and I get to keep working. How fair is that?'

Jocasta rocked back against the fridge and looked wistfully into the middle distance. 'You know what we need? A schoolies week for the mothers. As a reward for all we've been through. Straight after the exams. Somewhere inland, while all the eighteen-year-olds are at the coast. Somewhere with plenty of wine. And massages. I think the Hunter Valley would be perfect. Or perhaps the Victorian Alps.'

That's what I like about the HSC. It leaves everyone so focused. Ever since this time, the mood has been hectic, as Batboy and friends argue about which town they should subject to their invasion, while Jocasta rings around soliciting other takers for her schoolies week for mums.

Six days into our first brew, and by God I need a beer.

Better than sex

The way some of my friends talk about food, you'd think it was better than sex. Most of them have long ago stopped buying *Playboy* and *Penthouse*; instead they subscribe to *Gourmet Traveller* and *Delicious*. Apparently, they sit up in bed with their partners, reading these magazines, pointing out the weird new techniques and having a good hard look at the pictures. Sometimes, staring at a photo of Stephanie Alexander's lamb roast, they lean close to their partner and whisper in her ear, 'Darling, we really should try this one day — look what she's done with the garlic cloves.'

Some of them have Jamie Oliver videos hidden near the telly; recipes by Neil Perry in the bedroom drawer ready for 'perusal'; and catalogues from The Essential Ingredient and Cook's Paradise featuring all the weirdest gear. Brushes. Grill racks. French ovens. The government should forget the internet and start regulating this lot.

Still, if the *Penthouse* generation is now buying *Delicious* and *Gourmet Traveller*, then these magazines should at least face reality. Maybe a letters column would help.

☿

Dear Foodhouse,

I've never written to a magazine before, but what happened last night was really amazing. I'd pulled out some chops from the freezer to cook for my partner when she came home from work, but what a surprise she had for me. I knew I was in for something special when I saw the delicatessen bag on her arm, swaying from side to side, the light catching the David Jones Foodhall logo. Up the steps she came. I was right to be excited. She'd bought saffron-infused calamari for two. I cooked, we both ate, I had a cigarette and fell into a blissful slumber.

When we woke up, she talked about inviting her friend Sandra over next time — that way we could do it all again but this time together. I counselled against. Less calamari for me.

Blissful, New Farm, Qld

☿

Dear Foodhouse,

I'm a thirty-year-old account manager for a city advertising firm. Until last month I'd never discussed home cooking with anyone other than my husband, but all that stopped when I met Philip, a young graphic artist working at our agency. It started when he mentioned a recipe for veal. I went home that night and tried it with my husband. He loved it. Now almost every day Philip comes by my desk and mentions a new recipe.

He'll tell me the ingredients and method, then describe what the experience of eating will be like. Oh, the words he uses! The vegetables glistening and firm. The meat succulent. The stuffed aubergine exploding, the contents errupting from the case.

Each night I cook the dish but the experience of eating it is never quite as good as hearing Philip's description. I'm left curiously flat, out of sorts with both myself and my husband. This leaves me hungry for the next day when I know Philip will come past once again. Today, he's describing a Mussel and Fish Soup from Elizabeth David's French Provincial Cooking. *I can't wait.*

On Edge, Leichhardt, NSW

☿

Dear Foodhouse,
Just the other week I came home to discover my husband watching another cooking video. When we were first married he only had a couple of these. Now he's got a whole drawer full. It's making me embarrassed to cook, as my dishes never look as good as the ones in the videos. What's worse is my husband is now pressuring me to copy some of the techniques he's seen on screen. It's not that I mind doing the Jamie Oliver recipes, but I'm uncomfortable talking in the cockney accent when serving up. Is it just me, or should I say no?

Worried, Ringwood, Vic

Yes, these magazines represent a disgraceful world of unbridled emotions. But some people have turned away from both sex and food in order to embrace an even darker passion. Sleep, friends constantly tell me, is the new sex.

They just can't get enough of it. So why isn't there a dedicated magazine?

♀

Dear Sleephouse,

I want to tell you about an experience my wife and I have every Sunday night. At about 8.30 we start watching the latest bonnet drama on the ABC, but within about half an hour we are both at it — fast asleep in our armchairs. Naturally, we have a normal married life, sleeping in a conventional bed; but there's something so special about these Sunday night sessions. Maybe it's doing it in a chair. Maybe it's the way it's so spontaneous. Maybe it's the sense of abandon, as you give yourself over to the intense desire to sleep. I don't know, but we both agree it's satisfying like no other sleep.

Mr Sleepy-Head, Norwood, SA

♀

Dear Sleephouse,

I know jealousy is a curse but I want to tell you about my husband, Tom. He travels to work by train, an hour and a half each way, and I'm convinced he's getting some sleep when I'm not around. I've got two children and a busy job closer to home; by 5 p.m. all hell is breaking loose. I'm supervising the homework, getting dinner ready and sorting out my own work stuff. Imagine my surprise when a neighbour told me that he saw Tom on the train — catching up on sleep, as brazen as anything. I think a marriage is a partnership, and I don't like the idea of Tom getting his bit of sleep on the side. I've put my allegations to Tom, but he denies everything — saying he just had 'his eyes closed, while he thought through some office work'. I think he's lying but how can I be sure?

Suspicious, Blackheath, NSW

♂

Dear Sleephouse,
I keep fantasising about the sorts of sleeps I used to have when I was a young man, when I was aged sixteen and seventeen, sleeps that used to just go on and on and on, maybe for ten or eleven hours in a row. These days I can't even manage four hours of consecutive sleep; I'm always waking up and padding up the hall to go to the loo. It wasn't like that when I was a young fella! I used to do it everywhere — on the lounge, in an empty bathtub, even, on one memorable occasion, on a trampoline in a girlfriend's backyard. Today these are just memories, but when I wake up in the middle of the night I let my mind drift back to those times and sometimes I get sleepy all over again.

Dreamer, Subiaco, WA

Even weirder are those middle-aged men who are into neither sleep nor food. They have their own passions. The passions of the middle-aged bloke. If everyone else is to get a glossy publication, they shouldn't miss out.

♂

Dear Blokehouse,
I've never written to a magazine before, but I wanted to tell you about an experience I had recently, going away for the weekend

with two other couples. When we arrived, we set up the tents and started drinking — the men with beer, the women downing cans of rum and coke. By about ten o'clock we were all quite smashed and the women put on some really funky music for dancing. It was then I noticed that my Esky was a lot better packed than the Eskys brought by the other guys. The beers and ready-mixes were still really cold coming out of my Esky, something that couldn't be said for the others.

Partly it's the way I pack it, but also the way I insist no one opens the lid for long. I always jump up and yell 'Shut the lid!' if anyone even walks close to my Esky. Plus, I have a rule about people helping themselves to drinks — something I usually police with some vigour. While the others danced and occasionally made out with each other, I kept an eye on the Esky and was well rewarded. By the next morning my frozen orange juice packs were still rock hard. It was certainly a night to remember.

Mr Cool, Darwin, NT

desirable

The Fabulon would
communicate directly with
the primitive parts of the
woman's brain. Once alone
with her man, she'd find
herself rashly removing her
clothes, throwing them
dramatically in the corner,
before begging the bloke, in
her throatiest voice, to
gently launder them all.

A message from SexyBoy

Jocasta is standing outside our bedroom door mocking me. I'm on the phone in the hallway, leaving a voicemail message. 'Hi,' I say. 'Remember to put that book in your bag.' And then: 'Bye now.' It's a simple enough message, but I find my voice has gone all tender and sultry. The 'Bye now' is intimate, almost caressing.

That's why Jocasta is laughing. The message is to myself; I'm leaving it on my work voicemail. Jocasta says the man on the other end of the line must be called SexyBoy, since I'm talking to him as if I'm deeply in love. I hang up and she comes up full of tender concern. 'How was SexyBoy tonight?' she asks. 'Is he well? I know you two care a lot for each other.'

Fair cop, I suppose, but what tone of voice are you meant to use when addressing yourself on your own voicemail? Businesslike? 'Put that book in that bag and don't forget.'

Brusque? 'Book, Bag, Bye.' Or emotional? 'I've rung again because you're the only one who understands me. Please help by putting that book in your bag.'

Other questions crowd in. Should you say hello when it's you on the other end of the line? And how do you sign off? Hanging up on yourself seems dysfunctional; and yet saying 'See you later' suggests a touch of Sybil.

There's a similar dilemma once I get to work. I park my car and head for the stairs. When you emerge at the bottom, there's a large panel of mirrored glass. It's your last chance, having rushed to get to work, to check if you've remembered to put on your pants. Yet I know it's a two-way mirror, and the man inside the ticket booth is on the other side. He watches as each person steps from the stairs and he sees them flash the mirrored self a look of either admiration or despair.

I imagine his mordant commentary. 'You're not *that* good, champ.' Or 'I agree, love. The stretch top was a mistake.'

I know he does this because we had the same sort of panel in my father's newsagency. I spent much of my adolescence stacking papers in the back room and, when I looked up at the panel, I would see people staring fixedly at themselves. We had a display of maps just above the mirror and they'd pretend that's where they were focusing. Every day a score of people were absolutely engrossed in the map of Braidwood and Area 1:100,000. Their heads were tilted up towards the maps; but their eyes were angled down. A few, the younger ones, looked like they had just spotted their own SexyBoy or SexyGirl. They gazed at themselves with bedroom eyes. 'Absolutely gorgeous,' they were saying inwardly, the thought bubble pulsating into the shape of a heart. Most, though, just stared into the mirror with a sort of grim sigh, the way that you might look at a dog which had badly let you down.

I have the same problem at the car park. I want to look but I don't want to be caught. I pretend I'm staring at the glass itself rather than my reflection. Just as people in shopping centres pretend they are looking at the window display when, in fact, they're checking out themselves. I'm hoping the guy will assume I'm an expert in German mirrored glass and am trying to figure the precise origin of the stuff he has fitted. Meanwhile, I rapidly tick off my preparations for the day. My tie is on. I have remembered to rinse the shampoo from my hair. I have pants on.

I trudge down the road and into the lift at work. I wait to see if anyone else will get in with me. As we all know, catching a lift is a very different experience according to whether someone else gets in or not. With two of you in there, the lift is the most sombre place on earth. It's like a funeral. You gaze at your feet. Or stare, fascinated, at the lift's number display. ('Actually, I'm an expert in German lift mechanisms and am trying to work out this one's precise origin.') But have a trip on your own and it's twelve seconds of Dionysian abandon. Twelve seconds of burping, singing, dancing, mirror-staring and crotch-scratching — all of it ending just half a second before the doors slide open to reveal the model citizen, facing forward, arms loose, shoulders held high, ready to start his work day. A man so calm and poised he looks as though he's never scratched a crotch in his life. Well, certainly not his own.

By the time I finally get to my desk, I'm exhausted by the deceptions of the morning. How pleasing that the light on my answer machine is flashing. My heart races. I don't want to hope too much, but I think it may well be a message from *him*.

The eroticism of housework

For decades, the adolescent Australian male has pondered the ads for pheromones — the spray-on female attractant on offer for the unbelievably low price of $44.95. This stuff, it is said, attracts women much like a flowering shrub attracts a swarm of bees. The adolescent male is not stupid. He is suspicious of the claims being made. He realises it would take a strong chemical indeed to blind women to his own rather obvious faults, which currently include a fresh plague of pimples, chewed fingernails and a voice that breaks in the middle of multisyllabic words (which, luckily, remain rare).

On the other hand, there's the idea of being swarmed by unaccountably randy women, an image which tends to play on the mind of the adolescent male. Within days, hours, or more usually seconds, he finds himself filling in his cheque/money order/credit card number and sending off the order.

The product, of course, is a total failure: merely making the young man smell like a pig wrapped in plastic. This brings a distrust of society and its institutions which can last a lifetime.

But now new research from America shows where we went wrong. Instead of paying big money for the pheromones, we should have invested in a can of Fabulon. A quick squirt behind the ears and women everywhere would have been ours.

The research comes from Dr John Gottman of the University of Washington in Seattle. Having interviewed thousands of couples, Gottman has determined that men who share the housework are considered more sexually attractive by their partners. The story has had a huge run in newspapers around the world, usually under the banner headline: 'Housework Gives Men Sex Appeal: Study', which shows you just how many women are now running major newspapers.

Jocasta, along with women worldwide, has cut out the article and placed it on our fridge. She has always believed in the sex–housework link — and currently lists her erogenous zones as comprising the kitchen floor, the back bathroom and the lint filter in the spin dryer.

According to Jocasta, women are not turned on by Iron Men; they're turned on by Ironing Men. The strong hands flinging the ruched dress onto the ironing board; the delicate fingers separating the material so the iron can do its work; the heat of the iron; the smell of the Fabulon — it's all a heady mix. Televise the Ironing Man contest from the Gold Coast and she'd be watching.

If only men knew the secret: before every date they

should simply douse their bodies with Fabulon. Unlike pheromones, it really *would* act on a woman's subconscious — the Fabulon communicating directly with the primitive parts of her brain. Once alone with her man, she'd find herself rashly removing her clothes, throwing them dramatically in the corner, before begging the bloke, in her throatiest voice, to gently launder them all.

You can imagine the advertisement up the back of *People* magazine: *'You've probably noticed how some guys seem to get all the girls — even guys who are not that great looking. Now you know the truth — those guys are probably wearing Fabulon.'*

The only problem may be with quantities, since men usually operate on the theory that the more you use of a product the better it will work. Tell them that a squirt of spray starch behind the ears may attract women and you'll soon have blokes emptying two cans' worth down the front of their jocks. Apply a little heat and who knows what will happen.

And yet, just when this army of men is reaching for the Fabulon, undoing their jeans and preparing to empty out a couple of cans, along comes another piece of American research. While Dr Gottman has been studying sex and housework at the University of Washington, his colleagues at the University of Massachusetts have had a tighter focus. Following years of analysis, they have discovered that married women delay the menopause by two years, compared to those who are single. The difference, according to the researchers, is due entirely to their constant exposure to male pheromones — not the ones purchased through magazines, but rather the simple scents secreted by their husbands' sweat glands.

Men, it seems, need do nothing more than lie on the couch and give off odours and already we are socially useful.

For years women have delivered the shouted challenge to their menfolk: 'How come you're just lying on the couch, stinking the place out?' But no longer is this the insult it once was. 'Exactly,' we shall answer as one, 'and couldn't you show a bit of gratitude?'

Some women, it's true, remain unconvinced about the utility of having a man around. 'Sure, I'd like to put off the menopause for two years; but are there any other good reasons to invest in a man?'

The answer is yes. Largely because men will do anything for sex.

If men had a calling card, it would probably read:

The Male of the Species
Quick repairs
Companionship
Pheromone secretion
'We'll do anything for sex'

But there must be more to recommend us than the fact we stink. Well, you're right: there is more.

Killing rodents. Women, of course, are quite capable of killing rodents, but many see this activity as a useful opportunity to keep their bloke in touch with his tribal masculinity. Evolution has trained man to hunt down bison and buffalo, kangaroo and emu, and then to kill them in a frenzy of bloodlust. Yet opportunities for this sort of action are rare if you live in a flat in North Ryde or Chadstone.

Killing a cockroach with a rolled up copy of *Men's Health* will just have to do. Watch your man! Applaud your man! Draw a halt only when he suggests mounting his victim on an oak plaque above the fireplace.

Heavy Lifting. The workplace safety people have developed all sorts of complex codes about what weights can be lifted safely, according to the size of the bloke. All ignore the fact that each bloke has two weight-lifting modes: (1) on his own; or (2) watched by women. A man who will struggle to shift a pot plant on his own will find himself able to lift the back of a car when observed by a group of women. Yes, this will be followed by a lifetime of agonising back pain, but it's well worth it for four seconds of passing admiration.

Putting out the garbage. Why is this a male task? Because it used to involve heavy lifting (see above) and thus it became 'a gendered task'. Am I the only one who has noticed the bins now have wheels? Somehow, the 9.2 million women in Australia are yet to notice. Luckily, men do not mind dealing with smelly garbage. Nor with compost. Perhaps we realise it all adds to the delightful odour we give off when relaxing on the couch.

Speaking of which, only now is it clear why the production of odour has been so important to men over the generations. We hadn't realised that, deep down, we are merely trying to be of medical assistance.

Breathe it in, women. Not only aromatic; also good for you. Add a squirt of Fabulon to the already intoxicating cocktail and, frankly, you won't be able to help yourself.

Bo-Bo erectus

I feel sexier. More primitive. I prowl the kitchen, looking for my mate. I spot Jocasta by the toaster, trying to fish out an English muffin that has become stuck. She is dressed, alluringly enough, in spotty pyjamas and ugh boots. I growl and beat my chest. 'Come on, baby. You haven't the time for muffins. Marriage is about procreation. It's about the survival of the species.'

Politicians both here and in the US have been talking about gay marriage. We can't allow gay marriage, said both the Prime Minister and the President, because marriage is about the continuation of the species. Suddenly, ever since they spoke, I see myself in a new light, as the last of my species, swinging from tree to tree. I am the last of a mighty line, the last large-arsed male Bo-Bo still alive in the jungle. I must find another large-arsed Bo-Bo and breed. 'Come on,

Jocasta,' I say, leaning closer. 'We must multiply, for marriage has no point without procreation.'

'I've already multiplied,' she mumbles distractedly, 'and now I want some breakfast.'

'But Bo-Bo want to breed. Bo-Bo want species to continue.' I beat my chest but to no avail. Sometimes I suspect Jocasta takes no notice of the Prime Minister at all. Nor the President. 'Poor Bo-Bo,' I mumble, stumbling out into the backyard in order to urinate against a tree.

So many species have become extinct, but until now I'd never spotted the connection with gay marriage. The dodo. The Tahitian sandpiper. The Tasmanian tiger. Presumably all of them, at one point or another, relented and allowed gay marriage. Next thing: *poof*. The whole species gone. The Mauritian flying fox. The Tongan giant skink. The spectacled cormorant. All victims of gay marriage.

Take the mystery of the dinosaurs. For millions of years they dominated the earth. And then suddenly they were extinct. The Prime Minister and the President may be the first to have solved the mystery. The dinosaurs must have allowed gay marriage. A few years on and the whole institution of dinosaur marriage was sapped of meaning. The straight dinosaurs began standing around in ugh boots, toasting muffins and forgetting to procreate.

It takes a pretty special Prime Minister to understand this sort of hidden evolutionary history. We are indeed a lucky people.

Certainly I'm starting to see Jocasta in a new light. She is not so much a woman as the bearer of her evolutionary history. 'You are primeval slime,' I say to her, 'phylogenically speaking.'

'There's no need to talk like that, just because I won't come across,' she responds, with a mouthful of muffin.

'No, it's wonderful,' I continue. 'You were slime which then divided asexually. You turned into a tiny sea creature, clambered onto land, grew wings and experimented with flight, then evolved into a mammal.'

Jocasta takes another bite of toast. 'No wonder I'm tired.'

'Only recently,' I continue, 'have we learnt to walk erect.'

'Well,' Jocasta says, staring at my pyjamas and pointing with her muffin, 'you don't seem to be having trouble in that regard. Not this morning.'

It's true that I, Bo-Bo, stand ever-ready to attempt the continuation of the species. In the past some males have been embarrassed by this ever-readiness. But no longer: not since the Prime Minister and the President explained what marriage is all about. I look downwards and what I see is now bathed in a sort of heroic light. In my mind's ear, I hear trumpets playing. A choir of angels sings off to the side.

'The Prime Minister is right,' I say to Jocasta. 'The very species, it depends on me. It depends on *this*.' I gesture downwards, hoping she will share my sense of awe.

Somewhere in the mind of men always lurked this knowledge. We knew *it* was the centre of life itself; a thing not only of beauty but of historical importance. For years we had shown it to others, hoping they would see it in the same way. Backlit somehow. Significant. Inspiring. But instead there was constant disappointment. Constant mockery. There were those who laughed. Those who crinkled their noses in distaste. And those many who just let loose a disappointed: 'Oh, is that all.' Until now.

'Bo-Bo is but a tool of evolution,' I say to Jocasta tenderly.

'Certainly Bo-Bo is a tool,' she says, popping the last of the muffin into her mouth.

'But marriage has no point without constant procreation,' I say. 'The Prime Minister says so.'

Jocasta slings her plate in the sink and heads to work. 'Personally, I'm not surprised the Prime Minister thinks it's a good idea. He's been doing it to the country for years.'

I, the noble Bo-Bo, the last of my species, take that to be a no. I slink out the back to once more urinate against a tree. It seems that, yet again, the species will have to wait. Right now, I'm just not in a position to save it.

Knot trying

I always hated the Boy Scouts, mostly because they made me sleep in the ditch. The ditch was dug around the edge of the tent to stop water coming in. As the youngest, newest and most incompetent recruit, I got to sleep on the edge of the tent and would soon end up in the ditch. It was uncomfortable, demeaning and — following heavy rain — gave fresh meaning to the term 'floating off to sleep'.

I also had a problem with the flying fox (foolishly dangerous), the hygiene standards (appalling) and the fact that our holiday camp was shared with every young blowfly in the country. Maybe their parents didn't want them hanging around home during the holidays either.

Naturally, I'd have rather stayed in my bedroom at home and got on with my reading, but my parents had determined that a week sleeping in a ditch might be of assistance in the cause of achieving some sort of conventional manliness. It was, I guess, a last-ditch attempt.

Most baffling of all were the knots. I could never follow these intricate patterns of right over left, and left over right; of hitches and half pikes and slips. I would stick out my tongue and try to follow the diagram. Quickly, I'd find my tongue knotted while the rope lay limply in my hand: a metaphor for failed manhood if ever there was one.

And did one really need forty different knots in order to survive for a week on the coast? Certainly the explanations seemed a little far-fetched. The cat's paw was good for attaching a rope to a hook, should one wish to achieve such a connection. The clove hitch was good for tying sacks, although the camp was sack-free, so who could be sure? And the bowline was excellent for tying around someone in a dramatic river rescue. (Just hold still in the raging torrent for three hours, while Richard, with his tongue stuck out, tries to follow the diagram. Just two hours and fifty-five minutes quicker, and I could have saved that boy's life.)

Why have these nightmares come back to haunt me nearly four decades on? I blame the people next door. There's a black-tie function on this weekend and I've bought tickets for myself and Batboy. I mention this to my neighbours, Jenny and Tom Neatwhistle, and Tom says: 'I hope you'll be wearing a proper hand-tied bow tie, and not one of those pre-done ones.'

I confess I'd planned to hire a couple of suits with built-in clip-ons, but the confession leaves my neighbour aghast. As with the Boy Scouts and their wretched knots, it seems there's an issue of masculinity here.

'Think of the moment,' Tom confides, 'late in the night, when people are starting to relax. You'll undo your top button and then pull the ends of your bow tie. The knot will fall out, and the ends of the tie will dangle against your pressed white shirt. All the women will melt. They'll know you are the real deal; that you are master of your own bow tie; that your fingers have a certain, ahem, dexterity.'

I enjoy this vivid portrait of myself and a table of fawning women. I enjoy it so much that I race out the next day and purchase real bow ties for myself and for the boy. At both David Jones and Gowings I notice they have three dozen pre-tied models, displayed beautifully, and a single choice of tie-your-own hidden on the bottom shelf. My hand hovers: why are the real-deals so unpopular? Could it be that they are harder to tie than one might think?

I reason with myself: silly old duffers have managed to do this for centuries; how hard can it be? We buy the ties and head home. Once there, we print off a diagram from the internet and set to work, both standing in front of the mirror. I discover that while I was completely hopeless at tying knots at age nine, I'm even worse now. Batboy, if this is possible, is even less skilled. Being seventeen, he also loses his temper in a more spectacular fashion.

The suave James Bond atmosphere we were hoping to create seems rather distant as we stomp in front of the mirror, swearing and sighing, petulantly scrunching our faces and declaring the whole thing 'a bloody joke'.

For three nights we practise. Occasionally, through blind luck, we achieve the sort of granny knot with which a five-year-old might tie his or her shoes. The rest of the time we get nowhere.

We're so desperate I finally remember being told about an old trick: the tie-substitution racket. You arrive wearing a clip-on, then whip out to the loo towards the end of the evening. You remove the clip-on and substitute it with an untied real-deal, just dangling it around your neck. The women, it is said, will assume it's been real all the time and begin their incessant fawning.

It's an evil idea but it may be our only hope. Either that or we'll stitch ourselves into sacks and throw ourselves into a raging river, thus giving ourselves an excuse to not go. Anybody know how to do a clove hitch in a hurry?

Symbolically clean

With all the effort going into fashion, couldn't they focus a bit more on the care instruction labels? Does anybody understand what they mean, with their series of triangles, crosses and encircled washing machines? And do they have to be quite so alarming?

With particularly skimpy outfits, the care instruction label is now bigger than the garment. The garment must be hand-washed, in lukewarm distilled water, and then placed on a flat surface in the shade. Whatever you do, don't squeeze it or wring it. And, certainly, never even mention the word 'dryer' in its presence. If you must speed up drying, you may blow on it gently, providing you haven't recently eaten anything spicy. Once it's dry, place your iron in the next room and simply walk past the doorway to that room, with the garment on a hanger, gently encouraging it to de-wrinkle.

The little diagrams on the care label are full of drama and intrigue, especially as one can only guess at their meanings. Does the picture of the choppy water mean you can only wear the garment sailing? What is this mysterious black hand being plunged into the choppy water from above, and this thing that looks like a croissant with a giant cross through it? And why, next to it on the label, is there a picture of a square window filled with prison bars? Has someone stolen a croissant, jumped into the ocean to escape, but then been caught and locked up? The care instructions on my new pants have more plot development than the average airport thriller.

Even worse are those garments that are beyond washing. They are so delicate, the manufacturer cannot begin to suggest how you might clean them. Even purchasing laundry powder while wearing them may invalidate your rights under consumer law. 'Dry Clean Only' is the label's terse instruction.

Typically these garments are pure wool — maybe a suit or a pair of pants — and of course there's no way wool can be exposed to water. Frankly, I find this a little hard to believe. Last time I looked, the sheep in the fields were not wearing raincoats. They were not marching around with a stockman holding a dainty little brolly over each animal. If the label is right, and wool shrinks when wet, why doesn't it do it when it's on the sheep's back? Why haven't we got a whole nation of size sixteen sheep waddling around in size fourteen fleeces? Why don't they pant and wheeze while gambolling in the field, rather like a fat man over-optimistic in selecting his size of Levi's?

I'm convinced it's all a rip-off involving the dry cleaning industry and secret payments to the wool growers. Just tell them they can't be washed,' the dry-cleaners hiss, while handing over the cash to some bloke in an Akubra. 'If they want them cleaned, tell them it's got to be done *dry*.'

But here's the thing: how can cleaning really be 'dry' anyway? Try taking a dry shower and see how clean you get. If your toddler, after using the loo, claimed to have dry-cleaned his hands, would you believe him? My hunch is that the big high-tech machines dominating the dry-cleaner's store are just a cover. The whole thing is a scam. Out the back of the shop there's some sort of creek. They have people out there, crouched over the water, beating your new Armani suit with a rock. Hours later, they bung it on a hanger, wrap it in plastic, and no one's the wiser. 'Thank you, wool industry.'

Surely it's time we give up the fiction and admit that everything should be just thrown into the machine and thence into the dryer. That way the warning labels would be free for more useful messages.

Warnings labels such as: 'You? In our stuff? You must be joking.' Or: 'Think again, lady.' Or simply: 'Ha, ha, ha.'

The trick is making the label match the product. On a Bonds T-shirt, for instance: 'Arm ribbing may make upper arms appear fat.' On a pair of pants from Jeans West: 'Danger of self-wedgie in some models.' Or on a dress in the window of a Paddington boutique: 'May look sensational on the plastic hanger, but appalling on anyone heavier than a plastic hanger.'

Most of all, customers need to be warned about what happens once they leave the shop. 'Bum may sag after moderate use.' 'Pants will look good when standing up in the change room but will later develop piano-accordion crotch.' Or on a pair of $800 shoes: 'Will stink after one outing.'

Maybe these sorts of messages are already there — hidden within the care instructions. Suddenly that picture of the crossed-out croissant doesn't seem so obscure. 'Eat more than one of these each year,' the label is telling you, 'and you'll never fit into this garment ever again.'

How to write a book

With so many writers' festivals on these days, many readers have contacted me wondering how they might become authors, so as to be invited to the high-level soirees currently on offer. Happily, it doesn't seem too difficult.

Remember, these notes are only a basic guide. You'll also have to employ a good publicist.

Procrastinate. This is an essential part of the writing game. There's nothing like commencing a novel to make housework appear a joy. Just sitting down and typing the words 'Chapter One' can make tackling last night's washing-up look very attractive. Hanging out the laundry becomes a task that has to be done this very minute. Ditto cleaning out the bits of rice and meat stuck in the kitchen-sink strainer. Certainly it took Flaubert seven years to write *Sentimental*

Education, but you should have seen his shower recess by the end of it. Absolutely sparkling.

Procrastinate some more. Having written your first sentence, sit back and marvel at its poise, economy and limpid intensity. Spend the next three hours mentally rehearsing your acceptance speech for the Nobel Prize for Literature. Be sure to decide who to thank, and who to rather pointedly leave out. Perhaps, like Patrick White, you should donate the proceeds to fund a prize in your own name? But should it be for young playwrights or for elderly poets? Spend some time considering the advantages of each before deciding that — no — you deserve all the money yourself.

Write second sentence. Here's where you start introducing your characters. Remember: the real skill in writing is avoiding too many 'he saids' and 'she saids'. This is what separates a class act (publisher's receptions, prizes, offers of sex) from a basic literary failure (ten boxes of unsold books beneath the bed). Consider having your characters make a physical movement each time they speak, so as to tip off the reader as to who is talking.

> Jason turned towards her: *'I think I'm falling in love.'*
>   Jacinta swivelled her face closer to that of her lover: *'I am too.'*
>   Jason turned his head sharply and looked towards the window: *'Are you? Are you really?'*
>   Jacinta jerked her head downwards to stare at her shoes: *'No actually, I think it's just wind.'*

Remember: if you are writing really fluidly, your characters should be in need of a chiropractor by the end of chapter one. By the end of the three-book deal, they'll both be in a neck brace.

Purchase a copy of *Yates Garden Guide*. In the real world no one knows the names of trees and shrubs, with the possible exception of the ABC's gardening host Peter Cundall. Yet — for reasons I don't understand — all the characters in novels are horticultural experts. No way can your main character walk past something described as 'a tree'; you need more detail. Even 'He walked past a big tree' won't please the literary types. He has to walk past 'a gnarled river gum', 'a sweetgum liquidambar' or perhaps 'a vigorous hedge of hibiscus just coming into flower'. Perhaps you've wondered what they do in all those endless creative writing courses? I'm convinced: mainly horticulture.

Add some fauna. Novelists not only know the names of trees and shrubs, they also — amazingly — know the names of birds.

> *Dressed in his chinos and striding purposefully through the early afternoon sunlight, Jason disturbed a flock of sulphur-crested cockatoos. They rose as one, their distinct screeching filling the crisp air, before they settled back into the branches of a struggling European beech. Next, Jason walked past a potted Murraya tree, about two metres tall and just coming into flower, the orange blossom scent hitting him like an invigorating slap. A kingfisher bobbed in the nearby water, hoping*

to catch the silver perch which live in this part of the harbour.

This is all very well, but how do they know these things? Whenever I read a passage like that I imagine the notes they must scribble in the margin of their manuscript: 'Note to self. Check these details. What is a kingfisher? Is it a bird, or actually a fish? Are there perch in the harbour? Does *Murraya* flower in autumn? If not, what other scents are available to hit Jason like an invigorating slap?'

Do make sure you remove such pencilled notes before submitting the manuscript to a publisher.

Purchase a thesaurus. We couldn't help but notice that you had Jason 'walking' back there. Clearly you have yet to purchase a thesaurus. Do so and immediately consult section 266: 'locomotion by land'. Next time we see Jason, we expect him to be trudging with the despair of a man who knows he has lost Jacinta's love for ever. Or alternatively moving with the carefree long strides of a man full of hope, through air heavy with the smell of hibiscus. If you're going for an overseas prize, you could even have him perambulating.

Add weather. According to novelists, the weather constantly reflects the emotional state of the characters. I have checked with the weather bureau, which describes this theory as 'extremely unlikely'. Still, it worked for Emily Brontë, so get stuck in. No way do you want your character running joyously down George Street only to notice that around him the sky is full of anger, the day dark as a cave, the wind keening its lovesong of loss and desolation. I mean: 'He laughed merrily as the rain lashed his darkened, windswept figure,' is just not going to work. If in doubt, invest in a copy of *Wuthering Heights* and plagiarise Emily's weather.

Throw in brand names and food. People in novels love describing food. Apparently it's a great way of keeping the sex scenes apart. They also love using brand names in a way that people in real life rarely do.

> 'Let's just take it slowly,' said Jason, touching the back of her Versace capri pants, while she placed her hand on his freshly pressed Max Mara chinos.
>
> 'Do you think,' she said, unzipping him, 'that normal people make a note of the brand and type of clothes they're removing, as they remove them?'
>
> 'Probably not,' he replied, removing his pince-nez. 'But I don't even know what pince-nez are, so here's hoping I'm removing the right thing.'
>
> Their bodies naked, the two embraced. Outside thunder clapped, and a train went over the bridge and into a tunnel. 'That was great sex,' she said with a satisfied sigh. 'Now, let's get ourselves some food. Something hot and really adjectival.'

Which brings us to the adjectives. In the real world, the person who makes your tuna sandwich is 'a young guy, nothing special really, just average looking'.

Mostly the sandwich tastes 'much like what you'd expect a tuna sandwich to taste like'. This is not the attitude which will get you invited to opening drinks at the Sydney Writers' Festival. We want a sandwich which will push along the plot, and a sandwich maker whose appearance will add to the novel's oppressive mood of despair. The sandwich maker should definitely be wearing a pair of Italian brown leather brogues. Or perhaps a pair of workman's Blundstones, worn down on one side in a way that indicates a limp: a sort of back story in a boot. Also, once your protagonist receives the tuna sandwich, make sure he eats it in the street outside. That way he can be dramatically killed by a falling tree branch, loosened by a bolt of lightning, the extreme weather curiously reflective of his state of mind.

Serves him right, I guess, for standing underneath a scarlet-flowered gum. With his horticultural knowledge, you'd think he'd know better.

We're all farmers now

I'm standing at the back door watching the clouds. They're dark enough. They could bring rain. But I've seen their like before. They tease you, then pass. Life's tough in the suburbs.

We're all farmers now. Ever since the water restrictions came in, we stand and watch the clouds. Will I do some hand-watering this morning or should I wait? What if I spent an hour hand-watering this morning only to have it rain tonight? I give my chin a contemplative rub and consider the clouds once more. It's the not knowing that can drive a man insane.

My eyes squint against the light as I survey the property. I stare towards the boundary fence, up to that distant back country, near the compost bin, where conditions are at their worst. They get a lot of sun up there. The country is steep, with some rough bricking around the clothesline. The rain, when there is any, doesn't have the chance to settle.

I push back the Akubra hat which I've taken to wearing and grimace against the heat. I look at the choko vine, curling limply over the fence. Production's going to be way down this year.

I wander up the road and pause outside the Charcoal Chicken. Some locals have gathered to talk, and naturally the conversation turns to the weather. There are blokes here who haven't washed their cars for three weeks. One old fella has lost a couple of prize rose bushes. Another missed the *Australian Idol* final on Wednesday.

'What were you doing, Terry?' we all ask, concerned.

He shakes his head grimly. 'Hand-watering. And the time got away from me. Before I knew it, the clock had gone 10.30 and I'd missed Jyssyntah's win. But at least the front hedge will be OK.'

Most say it'll rain tonight. Some say you can tell from the way the ants are swarming. Others swear by the behaviour of the local Sicilian grandmothers. If they're carrying umbrellas, then rain can't be far off.

Back home I move the pot plants out, rolling the big tubs from underneath the eaves. I'll let them catch any rain during the night, then roll them back first thing in the morning before the sun hits. With luck, I can keep the parsley going until next harvest.

I see Jocasta watching me as I work, her face etched with concern. It's always harder on the womenfolk.

We're still doing better than others in the district. Our neighbour, worried by evaporation, has installed a pool cover. The family used to have a whole menagerie of blow-up animals floating on that pool — giant pelicans, a sleek dolphin, a beautiful multicoloured swan with drink holders built into its wings. The day the pool cover was installed, they all had to go.

I asked my neighbour how he got rid of them, but he just went quiet and stared off into the distance, his hands buried in his pockets, his lips tight with distress. Sometimes, in the quiet of early morning, I'll hear gunshots from a distant suburb. Some other poor bastard has had to shoot his pool toys.

The waiting, the watching, the hoping. The sky to the east is dark. It looks like it's raining a few valleys away. Those lucky mongrels in Dulwich Hill and Marrickville. And here are we with nothing. A bloke can't just stand still and do nothing. I ride the boundary — striding out past the hot water heater and up towards the recycling bin. Just a couple of years back, the water would cascade down these steps. There'd be water everywhere — leave a bucket out, even a wine glass, and it would be full of water, mozzies breeding like crazy.

Not any more. I stare at the garden. Will any of the ferns be left by the end of summer? Who knows? And yet without the ferns the stone lion will look out of place, and the wooden Buddha thingy will look silly. If things get much worse, they'll have to move on.

And it's then, when my despair is greatest, when I'm cursing this unforgiving land and its harsh ways, that the first fat droplet of water hits my upturned face. Rain! The dark clouds hover, there's a crack of thunder, then Hughie sends it down, giant sheets of water lashing the ground, drumming on the red tile roof. Soon it's all flowing — great streams of water coming down the steps and pooling on the lawn.

Jocasta and I stand and watch as the rain sets in and the water begins to spread onto the back paving.

I push the Akubra back on my head and stare grimly out. 'Looks like we might be in for a flood.' I don't know. Here in the suburbs, it's either one thing or the other.

delusional

He goes to the top of the mountain, straps himself onto a small metal cafeteria tray, then hurls himself off the mountain. 'The winter is long,' he mumbles through ice-chapped lips, 'but death will be quick.' Three minutes later, horrified, he finds himself at the bottom of the mountain, alive, safe and having invented the sport they call 'the skeleton'.

Snow business

The northern winter is long and depressing. There are endless periods of enforced idleness, and much of daily life takes place in total darkness. Insanity is common, as are suicide and alcoholism. Perhaps this explains the sports featured in the Winter Olympics — all of which seem to involve new and ingenious ways of throwing yourself off a mountain.

Imagine you're in Finland and it's February. No one has seen the sun for months. And so Olaf climbs to the top of the highest mountain he can find, puts on his beloved skis and throws himself off. It's so cold, it's so boring, the vodka has all gone, he's thinking, 'I just want to die.' Miraculously, he lands upright on the skis and glides safely to the bottom. His suicide bid has tragically failed, but he's created the ski jump called 'the aerial'.

His friend Sven sees what happened to Olaf and is determined that his own suicide bid will not fail in a similar way. His vodka ran out weeks ago. He has only two rollmops left in his pantry. His wife ran off with a holidaying truck driver from Spain. So Sven takes no chances. He goes to the top of the mountain, straps himself onto a small metal cafeteria tray, then hurls himself off the mountain. 'The winter is long,' he mumbles through ice-chapped lips, 'but death will be quick.' Three minutes later, horrified, he finds himself at the bottom of the mountain, alive, safe and having invented the sport they call 'the skeleton'.

At a meeting that night, the citizens try to work out why people are throwing themselves off mountains — and yet constantly surviving. Says Hendrik: 'It may be because they can see where they are going.'

He suggests throwing oneself off the mountain, feet first, one's body strapped flat onto a board so one cannot see the track ahead. The next day, Hendrik gives it a try and finds himself at the bottom of the mountain, shaken but alive. Unbelievably, yet another Olympic sport has just been invented. This one they call 'the luge'.

The village now breaks into mass insanity. There's still nine months of winter to go, no vodka left, barely the smell of a rollmop, more Spaniards have come and departed with anyone good-looking, yet all the previously trusty methods of suicide are failing. The villagers take a vote and decide they'll just have to shoot each other.

Arming themselves with guns, they strap on their skis and stomp up the mountain, blasting randomly in both prone and standing positions. Some work in teams, some individually, while others blast while in pursuit. Tragically, no one dies. The villagers return depressed but alive. They discover they have invented the biathlon.

Some will argue that not *every* event in the Winter Olympics is life-threatening. They will give the example of figure skating. To which I will respond by mentioning Tonya Harding. They may then give the example of curling. To which I will respond that death from boredom is still death.

Again one struggles to imagine the moment the sport of curling was invented: the Finnish farmer inviting ten friends over to play carpet bowls, then realising he didn't have any bowls, nor any carpet. Even finding ten friends was hard going. But he did have some large rocks and a frozen pond, so maybe the seven who turned up could push the rocks from one end to the other then back again? 'Ah, Johannes,' his friends will all say, 'break out the rollmops. One snow-bound village, and now we've invented all the sports of the Winter Olympics.'

The war on error

For a month now, those closest to me have been acting most suspiciously. The government's anti-terrorist pamphlets have finally come in useful. The pamphlets remind you to look out for suspicious behaviour and suggest a list of purchases — including a radio, torch and latex gloves. I decide to throw myself into the war on terror.

6.15: With the coiled stealth of a panther I ease my upper body off the mattress and peer beneath the bed. If anybody is under there, they'll get the shock of their life. Thankfully, the coast appears clear. I check my bedside table. My 'kit' is still there in place. The battery-operated radio, the torch and the latex gloves. There's also my glass of water, across the top of which I've placed a strand of hair. With a flood of relief, I see the strand is still in place. We've survived another night.

6.17: I grab the torch and disappear under the doona, making a full visual inspection. Jocasta is asleep beside me, which leaves me wary. It's very difficult to assess whether someone has become a 'sleeper', especially when they are actually asleep. I pounce on her and give her a thorough check, paying especial attention to all possible hiding places. It has not escaped my attention that when I first met her she owned a T-shirt printed with a verse from the *Rubaiyat of Omar Khayyam*. Suspicious behaviour indeed, even for 1979.

6.18: Jocasta awakens and commences to shout, wriggle and even strike me about the face and head. I feel sure this indicates guilt. If a person's got nothing to hide, why should they object to a search? The alarm clock is about to go off so I disconnect it from the wall and throw it in a bucket of water. Jocasta says I am behaving oddly, which gives me pause to wonder just whose side she's on.

6.19: Decide to launch Operation Retrieve Morning Newspaper. Have some concerns about my neighbour who claims to be Irish but appears not to drink. This, I'm sure, is what the government means by a 'suspicious type'. I disguise myself by turning my dressing gown inside out and wearing a hat.

6.20: Gather up the paper in one long, crouched run, keeping my head down and the car between myself and my 'Irish' neighbour. Notice lack of grog bottles in his recycling. Irish, my arse!

6.21: I read out sections of the government's terrorist kit — telling Jocasta she should watch for someone buying large amounts of fertiliser. 'Perhaps you mean the Prime Minster,' she says. 'He's in possession of vast quantities of bulldust.' I make a mental note of her disloyalty and resolve to deliver a more thorough frisking.

6.22: I walk up the hallway armed with my tennis racquet. I pause in front of each door then jump into the room James Bond-style. All goes well, except for my leap into the living room, during which I land feet-first on the dog. The dog gets an appalling fright, as do I. My heart is pounding and I'm feeling strange pains up my left arm.

6.28: I've appointed myself chief warden of our street but have elected to keep the appointment secret from my neighbours (security reasons). I discover that the people next door have closed their venetians in a way that completely blocks my telescope. What are they up to? I decide to bring the whipper-snipper inside from the shed lest I need a weapon.

6.32: Jocasta appears rather truculent after this morning's frisking. I consult the fridge magnet for tips on how to handle her. Strangely, it provides no assistance whatsoever. Only when the dog walks past does she speak, inquiring as to why Darcy appears to be limping.

6.35: Using binoculars I spot my 'Irish' neighbour picking up his newspaper. He has recently grown a beard, even though it doesn't suit him. This strikes me as extra suspicious. His wife has also taken to wearing pedal-pushers, which are not even in fashion any more. I decide to plug in the whipper-snipper and set it going using a long extension cord.

6.40: 'It's all very well for us,' says Jocasta, studying the government's anti-terrorist fridge magnet, 'but what about people with the stainless-steel fridges. The magnets don't stick to them. Come a terrorist attack and the Smeg-buyers of Woollahra and Toorak will be completely unprotected. It will be a yuppie massacre.' Her tone is unhelpful and I make another note of her possible disloyalty.

6.41: Holding the whirring whipper-snipper in one hand, I lean a ladder against the back of the house and climb up in the hope of getting a better look at the 'Irish' neighbour and his wife. Naturally, I take the full anti-terror kit — grasping the torch between my teeth, the radio under one arm and wearing the latex gloves. Balancing the spinning whipper-snipper, I manage to train my telescope into my neighbours' bedroom, at which moment they look up, and spot me. Mine being an unofficial position, I rapidly deploy myself back to the ground, slipping in the process, and tumbling out of control — my terrorism kit flying from my hands.

6.45: Jocasta runs out to find me lying on the back paving, bleeding. The whipper-snipper is broken, the radio is in pieces and I have landed heavily on the upturned torch, which has inserted itself in a new home: one where the sun does not normally shine.

6.50: 'Good thing you've not become a victim of terror,' says Jocasta as she attempts to retrieve the torch. 'Still, I finally understand the need for the latex gloves.'

I make a further note of her unhelpful tone. She really is behaving quite oddly.

Show time

Every town in Australia has its rural show — shows such as the Royal Easter in Sydney, the Ekka in Brisbane and the Royal Melbourne. The only trouble with them is the educational side. Frankly, they are all a bit *too* educational. For years I've been trying to convince myself that steak comes in a packet from the supermarket and has nothing to do with those cute cows you spot in the distance when driving along the Hume Highway. Similarly, I like to pretend that a chicken burger has nothing to do with actual chooks (although, in the case of chicken nuggets, this may be true).

Then along comes the Show and wrecks everything. Young people ask uncomfortable questions about the next port of call for those sweet little piglets, all our illusions are shattered and everybody ends up in tears.

Since it's called a show, can't they put one on? I'd like to see new displays and exhibitions placing a more acceptable spin on the harsh world of agriculture. Surely a bit of bullshit isn't too much to expect from our farmers . . .

Mr Milko's Cows' Collective. At Mr Milko's we collect milk that has been generously donated from nursing cows keen to maintain their milk supply between calves. Individual cows choose how much to give, and receive certificates which they can later cash in on little luxuries such as molasses and starch. Naturally there is eager competition between cows about how much milk they give, with the winner usually boasting that she's 'better than the udder ones'. It's this sort of happy cow humour that keeps the industry sane — and growing. The milk is then placed in cartons made from recycled newsprint, oxygen-bleached in our factories by disadvantaged youth from struggling country towns.

The Stampede Meats Hoof and Hook Competition. All the cows employed by Stampede are themselves vegetarians but they understand this is not a choice for everybody. For generations, they've given their lives for this industry — but only at the time of their choosing. Our team of exit counsellors, headed by Dr Philip Nitschke, visits each cow in turn to make sure she is ready to go. Naturally some are uncertain and want to talk things over with Dr Nitschke. 'I haven't met a cow yet that doesn't want to chew the cud over the decision,' says the good doctor, 'but with my help they usually realise, much like my human patients, that now's the time to go.' Certainly, consumers can enjoy a steak or perhaps some sausages safe in the knowledge that a full and ethically sound process has occurred. The meat is packed in outback villages by refugees from oppressive regimes. It is pesticide-free and dolphin-safe.

Mr Fry-up's Pig Pen. The movie *Babe* is responsible for a lot of misconceptions about our industry. Some people, for instance, still believe that pigs are in some way harmed in the manufacture of bacon. Nothing could be further from the truth. Bacon is actually shaved off the animals in a process very similar to shearing. The product is then processed using salts collected on sustainable beaches by nomadic peoples in the Torres Strait Islands. Twenty per cent of all profits go to funding a pig-housing cooperative in the rainforests of Borneo. The product is completely sugar-free and diabetic-safe.

The Woodchop. Here at The Woodchop we only cut sustainable timbers grown on our own farms and harvested by transgendered stockmen displaced from the cattle industry. We fully accept the role of political debate in determining the future of our industry. That's why you'll see a greenie chained to each log in the arena. The axeman — or axewoman — must first approach the greenie and try to explain the sustainable basis of our industry and its role in keeping small towns afloat. Only once he — or she — has convinced the greenie to unchain him- or herself, using the simple force of logic, may the log be cut. This has extended the length of competitions from the old thirty-four seconds to an average three and a half months, but it makes for great suspense at the end. There is no fat or salt in our product. Our employees do not use plastic bags when shopping. Please use wood in moderation.

Showtime Dagwood Dogs. A vicious whispering campaign has been mounted against the whole dagwood dog industry, suggesting that our product contains meat trimmings swept from the abattoir floor and boiled up in month-old oil. Nothing could be further from the truth. Dagwood dogs are a naturally occurring food, eaten for centuries by the indigenous Conchita tribe in South America. The main part of the dog is an elongated bud from the Porchita tree, which we coat in hand-milled bran fibre. It is then sun-dried by indigenous rainforest tribes and reheated at the Show in our solar-powered ovens. It is GM-free and the stick is high in fibre. Should you wish to regurgitate our product, please do so responsibly.

Just joking

At the Museum of Contemporary Art there's a new exhibition featuring two traditional Greek busts, each sitting atop a plinth. A third bust has fallen from its perch and lies smashed on the floor. That's the idea of the art piece. It's called 'The Third Bust' and, walking from one gallery to the other, you are supposed to pick your way through the broken pieces.

There's a museum guard sitting nearby and instantly I have this great idea. I approach her with the twitching smile of someone about to unleash a particularly good joke and say: 'Gee, you haven't been doing a very good job! Look what's happened!' With a sweep of my arm, I indicate the shards of broken statue. She looks up with a gaze of unspeakable weariness. Suddenly I realise: she may have heard this joke before. From the look in her eyes, about forty-seven times and it's not yet lunchtime.

The union movement spends a lot of time agitating for workplace safety yet there has been no major study of the effect of Repetitive Joke Syndrome (RJS) on employees. Almost every job suffers from at least one Repetitive Joke. In this case I was the perpetrator. I have also been the victim.

Item: I am twenty-two years old and working as a waiter at the Sydney Hilton function centre. Each night I must serve a platter of fish balls, offering them to each patron in turn. Roughly seventy-three per cent of men and twenty-two per cent of women greet my offer of 'Would you like a fish ball?' with the response 'Pretty big fish'.

Item: I am twenty-three years old and working at David Jones' city store during the Christmas rush. I have scored the job operating the old-fashioned lift. Roughly 100 per cent of customers upon getting into the lift look at me and say: 'Gee, son, this must be a pretty up-and-down sort of job.'

Item: Psychologically devastated by these two experiences, I get myself a job in radio, whereupon people start greeting me with the phrase: 'Well, you've got a great face for it.'

When will the union movement face up to the damage that is being done? When will Worksafe Australia step in with some laws? Building sites are forced to display notices warning about safety hats and proper boots. What about a sign in the DJ's lift, or around the waiter's neck, saying: 'Hey, I've already heard it.'

Consider the state's police officers. Not only do they have to cope with violence and abuse. They have to cope with the

Repetitive Joke. Every time they go into a takeaway food shop it's the same: the two lads behind the counter spot the officers, point to each other and shout: 'He did it, officer. It was him.' And every time the police officers pause in the street, someone will say: 'He went that-a-way.' People wonder why police are leaving the force. It's not the wage rates. It's those bloody jokes.

Police are not the only victims. There are the people involved in making and selling bras ('Must be an uplifting sort of job!'); there are the barmaids ('I'd like two jugs, love, and have you got any beer as well?'); and there are people employed by councils under the title 'Noxious Weeds Officer' ('Oh, go on mate, you're not *that* bad!').

It's a social crisis that extends beyond the workplace. There are the people who are particularly tall ('What's the temperature up there, mate?'); there are people with odd names ('Mr Youngman? Well, you better grow up a little!'); and there are the people with lots of kids ('So have you worked out yet what's causing them?').

You could even list the world's most predictable witticisms in some sort of order ranked by the sheer compulsion people have to utter them. Here's a top ten based on some quick radio polling:

1. Seeing someone trip: 'Did you enjoy your trip?'
2. Seeing your neighbour washing his car or mowing her lawn: 'You can do mine next.'
3. Seeing someone in paint-splattered clothes: 'Did you get any on the walls?'
4. Meeting someone from a large family: 'Didn't your parents have a TV?'

5. Meeting someone with a name tag saying Pat: 'Is that a name or an instruction?'

6. On being asked if you've got a hearing problem: 'Eh?'

7. On being told someone has just flown in: 'Gee your arms must be tired!'

8. Meeting someone with a black eye or arm in a sling: 'How does the other bloke look?'

9. Reaching the front of the queue at the bank: 'Do you give any free samples?'

10. When a glass breaks at a party or at a pub: 'Taxi!'

Why is the psychological effect so great? Why does Repetitive Joke Syndrome reduce the most competent person to a seething wreck of resentment, hostility and misanthropy? The least I can do is to return to the Museum of Contemporary Art. I shall visit the security guard sitting next to 'The Third Bust'. I shall present myself and explain that I work in radio.

'Well, you've got the face for it,' she'll say instinctively, and at least we'll be even.

Flaunt it

Teenage boys are becoming anxious about their appearance, much like teenage girls. About eighty per cent of the boys in a new survey described themselves as unhappy with how they looked. At fifteen, they are spending $60 a month on hair and skin products. A quarter of them would like to have cosmetic surgery.

All this, I think, is a great shame. There are plenty of things that men can learn from women. How to pop a toilet roll onto the toilet-roll holder is just one example. But body image obsession is not one of them. Let me whisper to young men the secret of the tribe; the secret that has been passed from one generation of men to the next: we're just gorgeous, each and every one of us.

Next time you're at the beach have a good look around. There will be some gnarled old bloke striding along, massive beer gut held proudly in front of him, rather like the bow of a majestic sailing ship, his bald head pitted with skin cancers, his spindly legs buckling under his massive weight, his pair of budgie-smugglers sagging limply around his tiny and frozen member. And yet something about his gait reveals what he's thinking: 'My God, I'm a fine figure of a man.'

Yes, he's insane. But he's happy.

Meanwhile, coming the other way, will be the most beautiful woman, conventionally perfect in every way, but thinking to herself: 'I bet everyone's staring at my puffy ankles. How did they get so huge?'

She, too, is insane — unhappily so.

Why the difference? Why, when men get old and weatherbeaten, do they get called 'distinguished', while when women get old and weatherbeaten they get called 'old and weatherbeaten'? Why do men do year-long courses in Buddhism in an attempt to dissolve their ego, while women can achieve the same result in a three-minute tussle with a size ten dress in the change room at Target?

And why at the gym do the eyes of the men flick to their own best bit, staring lovingly at the one or two muscles they've managed to build, while the eyes of the women flick impulsively towards their one supposed imperfection?

Consider the matter of baldness. Who but a man would come up with the explanation that baldness is a sign of virility? 'Oh yes,' he'll say, running a hand through thinning hair, 'I've just got too much testosterone coursing through my system. I guess I've got more sex drive than other men.' As unlikely as this explanation seems, balding men have managed to convince the world it is a ridgy-didge scientific orthodoxy. Put the words 'bald' and 'sexy' into Google and you'll get 840,000 matches, kicking off with a website offering testimonials from women on the allure of bald men, 'Men of Perfection' T-shirts and a flashing message: 'I'm too sexy for my hair.'

If women commonly went bald, would they claim it as a good thing, offering it as proof of excess oestrogen? Would they start up websites and testimonial logs, and purchase 'Woman of Perfection' T-shirts?

Take the example of varicose veins. If women behaved like balding men, they'd claim varicose veins as a symbol of fertility. 'Oh, yes,' the woman would say, 'you get them in the later stages of pregnancy.' Here she would delicately unfold her legs and trace the throbbing purple lines with an outstretched finger. She would pause and flutter her eyelids: 'And, as you can see, I've fallen pregnant quite a few times.'

Again the point is not to mock the bald-headed men: they're the ones with the good attitude; they are the example we should all be following.

Certainly, it's difficult to imagine how these young men are spending $60 a month on grooming products. When I was their age, things were different — even when preparing for a night on the town. In terms of skin care, I'd get a handful of sugar, add it to some soapy foam and create my own abrasive face scrub. A firm hand would simply sandpaper away those troublesome pimples, leaving a bleeding and red-raw surface that singled me out in any crowd.

As for hair care, one rarely needed to purchase product. Far better to simply not wash one's hair for a given period. A week of not washing in order to achieve the David Bowie spiky look; a month and a half for the full-Elvis quiff.

'Ego,' as the band Skyhooks put it at about this time, 'is not a dirty word.' Today's generation of young men would be wise to remember it. And, hopefully, one day the girls will follow their wise lead.

I know I'm gorgeous. But so, you know, are you.

You must remember this

I remember the panic I'd feel when I was fifteen or sixteen: I'd walk into a party, spotting the mix of strangers and school friends. It was a sort of nameless dread, a mix of apprehension, shame, fear and desperate hope. Now, thirty years on, I walk into a party and still suffer nameless dread, but now it is literally so. This time round I can't remember anyone's name. Jocasta hovers by my side, like an old man's nurse, topping up my supplies as we go. 'That young guy is your son's soccer coach,' she whispers out of the side of her mouth. 'That woman in the corner is our dentist. That older lady coming towards us with her arms outspread, that's your mother.'

It's all very helpful. Within minutes my nameless dread starts to lift.

Then there's someone even Jocasta doesn't recognise. I smile and try to act friendly. I seem to know her *really* well, which may mean she was my girlfriend for all the years between sixteen and twenty-one or that she's the local vet. Do I kiss her on the cheek or shake her hand? Luckily, I've become expert at asking open-ended questions.

'How are you?'

'Fine. I hope your dog's recovered.'

I thank my lucky stars I didn't go for the kiss and quick grope. Quite acceptable with the ex, but enough to get you arrested with the local vet.

Of course, it's worse when you are meeting someone new. My problem is that I want to act friendly, remembering to smile, shake their hand politely and really look them in the eyes. Being vaguely human in this manner is clearly a big challenge, requiring 100 per cent of my concentration, since I inevitably walk away with no memory of their name. It could be Rumpelstiltskin for all I know.

Again I'm forced to employ certain stratagems.

'I might just grab your phone number. First, how do you spell your surname?'

'What? Smith?'

'Sorry, I meant your first name. I was having trouble with it.'

'What? Simon?'

By this time they think you are a little dim in the spelling department but perfectly friendly. A sort of jolly idiot.

Once you've captured their name, it's important to commit it to memory. A salesman I knew — sorry, I can't quite recall his name — favoured the technique of immediately repeating the name back to the person who's just supplied it.

'Well, Simon, I guess that's right, Simon, I can see what you mean, Simon.' This is fine, as long as their name is not

Auberon, Tristan or Kimberly-Sue, in which case they might think you're taking the mick.

Far better to develop a mental note. The guy with blond hair is John, so we repeat the sequence until it's locked in: 'blond' equals 'surfer' equals 'John'. Thus: 'Surfer John, Surfer John, Surfer John'. Depending on the identifying characteristic you choose, this method can deliver instant name recognition and solve all your social problems — or cause you to stride towards acquaintances with a welcoming smile, saying, 'Well, if it's not old Fatty Steve.'

But if I'm bad with names, I'm worse with numbers. I feel I've been asked to remember one PIN too many, as a result of which, I now cannot remember any at all.

It started with bank PINs some time in the early eighties. We were all given a four-digit number. Having used mine for twenty years, I now find myself — on the odd occasion — able to remember it. But these days it has competition. I have a four-digit PIN to play back my voicemail, and another one to make interstate phone calls. The valuables at work are stored in a cupboard with a three-digit code. Both my local video stores want a password. And the office computer wants a mix of letters and numbers, which it forces me to change every month. At the same time, there's a car park near work with six floors, each colour coded.

I begin each day mumbling as I walk, trying to commit it all to memory. I'm parked on Green 4. My phone PIN is 7338. My voicemail is 1803. The speed dial prefix is 82. And the names of my children will come to me if you just give me a minute.

There are other numbers. The car rego. My date of birth. The question of whether my younger boy is in Year 7 or 8.

I'm also keen to stay in touch with the fact that the Eureka Stockade occurred in 1854. It's the single fact I remember from six years of secondary schooling and so we have a sentimental attachment.

As with people's names at a party, I end up devising complex mnemonics. My phone PIN, for instance, is easy. Each time I want to make an interstate call, I simply imagine one of the two 3s in the middle was turned around and faced the other. This would make them look like an 8, which — by freakish chance — is the last number. Which is one more than the 7 at the beginning. I dial the PIN, repeating my mnemonic, the mirror image 3s pulsing before my eyes, and sigh with relief when I hear the number ringing. What a shame I can no longer remember who it was I dialled.

And so I attempt other methods. The floor of the car park is the same number as my child's class at school. My bank PIN is the same as the date of the Eureka Stockade, just backwards. Except for the middle numbers which, looked at right, remind me of two fat men dancing.

By the end of the day, my brain clanks as I walk. I'm pretty sure the Eureka Stockade happened in 1833 and my son is in class Green 8. My car must be parked on Oxford Street, as I'm sure I remember something about gay men dancing. I pause before the locked stationery cupboard. Is this the PIN which has something to do with the Eureka Stockade or is this the one connected to the fat men dancing? And if so, are the fat men dancing back to back (two 3s)? Or face to face (two 8s)? Or has each fat man now scored a thin partner (two 10s)?

I decide I can live without stationery. And without interstate phone calls. And who needs a computer? But at lunchtime there's no choice. My wallet is empty. I stand in front of the bank's cash machine, a queue steadily forming behind me. I attempt one number. And then another. There is muttering. 'What's he doing?' I hear someone say, and a blush of shame creeps onto my face. I'm PIN-numerate.

Sometime this week you'll be behind one of us. In the bank queue. At the video store. In the supermarket checkout. You'll think we are slow or mad or difficult. But no, we'll just be trying to remember our PIN and perhaps our own name. Have sympathy for our nameless, numberless dread. We've been asked to remember just one thing too many.

'24/7'

Only eighteen months ago the phrase '24/7' was in all the best places. Walk through the funkier clubs in New York or Paris, and you could always overhear someone mentioning '24/7'. It was the hip new nickname for 'twenty-four hours, seven days a week,' and everybody wanted to share a little of 24/7's limelight.

'I listen to music 24/7', they'd say. Or 'I like to work and play 24/7.' Or even 'Our company will deliver 24/7.' One minute you'd see 24/7 in a newspaper headline, the next on the lips of a film star. It was like a whirlwind. Everyone wanted a piece of 24/7. Yet in the midst of the adulation came a warning. Someone, 24/7 can't remember who, told the story of the phrase 'As-You-Do'.

'Oh, yes,' 24/7 was told. 'As-You-Do was popular. *Really* popular. It was the way As-You-Do could fit into every situation. A chat show host would be lost for words and instinctively he'd reach for As-You-Do. Say somebody was talking about a rock star and how he chucked up and then inhaled his own vomit. Straightaway the host could say: "As You Do," and suddenly the audience would be laughing and cheering. The embarrassing moment would be over. No wonder As-You-Do was so in demand.

'Almost every night, As-You-Do was on at least one of the TV chat shows — and always getting the really big laughs. Letterman, Leno, Parkinson, Rove. Sometimes all of them on a single night. Everyone loved to make use of As-You-Do.'

'So what went wrong?' asked 24/7, suddenly overtaken by this terrible queasy feeling.

'As-You-Do just became too popular. Kids thought As-You-Do belonged to them. So did office workers and cab drivers. The TV hosts and beautiful people didn't like it. They said As-You-Do was overexposed, overworked. "As-You-Do," they said, "has become a cliché." And, frankly, they were right.'

Listening to all this, 24/7 was choked with anxiety. To think people could be so fickle towards a fresh new phrase. Who would have thought it could be a crime to be just a little popular?

'So where is As-You-Do now?' asked 24/7, in a tiny, hesitant voice.

'Who knows? The last sighting was down on the coast, south of Sydney, at a rundown caravan park. Some young kids were using As-You-Do, one after the other, but it was all in the wrong context. One would say they'd just had lunch and the other would say "As-You-Do", which isn't even funny. Frankly, it's abuse.'

The knot of anxiety was tightening in 24/7's stomach. 'And to think,' the informant continued, 'As-You-Do had, at one stage, been considered for a prominent line in *Trainspotting*.'

Panic was now engulfing 24/7. Every time there was a new 24/7 headline, or a 24/7 website or a celebrity mentioning 24/7, it was a knife in the guts. Popularity was death.

With trepidation, 24/7 started doing research, trying to find out what happened to all the hip phrases of the past, after they left the limelight. It was not pretty reading. There was the first outing of Puh-lease on *Friends*. And of Yadda-Yadda-Yadda on *Seinfeld*. And of He-LLO on *Buffy*. Hilarious! The whole audience in stiches. Funniest thing ever. Then, six months on, dropped. Dagsville to even mention them.

Or what about the phrase 'All over town like a cheap shirt'? How everyone laughed on its first appearance. Three weeks later and it was all over town like a cheap shirt. Who's laughing now? Nobody, thought 24/7.

In the library, 24/7 continued working 24/7 on those older phrases. Oh, to see 'Just to the right of Genghis Khan' on those fabulous first outings. A few quality novels. The odd West End play. How people laughed! How they applauded! Then five years on it was TV sitcoms of middling quality; to be followed by an old age hanging around local council meetings and school P&Cs, being trotted out by thin-lipped ideologues and corrupt mayors.

The story sent 24/7 into a deep depression, right at the moment the really bad news came in. The same group of kids that had abused As-You-Do had now got hold of 24/7. They were using 24/7 almost hourly. In truth, 24/7 was relieved. The anxiety had been terrible. But now it was all over. Into the bathroom staggered 24/7, swallowing a handful of pills, chug-a-lugging a bottle of whiskey, then jumping from the tenth-floor window. As-You-Do.

Yadda-Yadda-Yadda — could someone spare some sympathy? 24/7 was only ever a phrase we were going through.

deranged

Once a person is deceased, a
lot of people might say: 'Fair
enough. He's worked hard —
time for a rest.' But here's
the point: do the dead have
the right to lie there,
sponging off the rest of us,
just because they've passed
into some other 'special
category'?

The Eleventh Commandment

Please forgive me, Father, for I have sinned. I am not fit to be part of this thrusting modern economy. I have sins of commission and omission to confess. I have failed to compare long-distance telephone options. There, it is said. And, behold, I have not used a calculator to study the choice of plans, thence to average the costs over the full length of the contract. Nor have I studied my bundling options.

And so it came to pass that my wife sayest: 'This Telstra bill is an abomination. It is steeped in vileness and evil. Shall we not compare other plans?' But I denied her thrice, smoting her with the words: 'We could compare plans or we could just do nothing. I can never be bothered with such hassles.'

Verily, I stand naked, without excuse for my words, apart from the sin of sloth, and the loss of my calculator, which I could not find in any of the drawers, even unto those in the shed. But help me, Father, for now I fear my beloved will runneth away with another man, one who can amortise a debt with one hand, while stroking her wild hair with another, and who could blame her?

Father, I have not compared superannuation funds. Judge me as you must. I have not studied the feature article in last week's Money section, nor have I checked my fund's average weighted returns against those of comparable funds, both under the three-year and five-year systems of averaging. Verily, when the statements arrive, do I place them on the raiment of the kitchen table and plan to look at them, but fast do I become sorely distracted and so I dispatch them to the box in the hall cupboard.

Father, I was once young and knew not what I did, but now I am old and I hath no excuse. I sit before you, festering with evil. Yet there is still more to confess. It came to pass last Tuesday that my neighbour, Tom Neatwhistle, spake to me over the fence, and, lo, he sayest that true and real savings are now available through a broadband internet connection, and verily did he give me pamphlets and an article from the *Bulletin* which described how to calculate one's current costs, including dial-up, and compare these with a variety of offers, many with full and ripe download limits.

Later, after the dinner begat the sitcom and the sitcom begat bed, I cast these offers before my countenance, but, lo, I found my eyes grew sleepy and verily did I discover that I just couldn't be knotted.

Choice is offered to me, all golden and shining, and yet do I turn my head in fear. Deals are there to be compared and yet I find myself limp with indecision. Send me asunder,

Father, for I have sinned. I am not equal to all that is offered by our gods.

May I come closer, Father? I have something to show thee. Can I admit it? My cheeks rage red with shame; tears sting the eyeballs which did not look and did not see. For five years and ten months hath I paid this Telstra bill, yet never hath I looked at the fine print: a charge of $3 per month for handset rental. Father, that handset stopped working six years ago. I threw it in a box in the laundry and bought a new one. I never knew I was still being charged for it because I never read the bill. I am full of regret now, of course, but remorse will never bring back that sweet $200.

Father, again I must creep closer and make my voice whisper so that it slithers towards you like a snake. It is of fantasies that I speak, dreams that come to me late at night, dreams of when I was a young man and had no choice. If I wanted a phone, I would ring up. Just like that. Not a thought in my head. One company, one plan, one price. Ohhhhh. There could be no regrets, for, verily, I had no choice but to do as I did. The bank also. One account, one choice, one rate. There were two airlines, but oh, wondrous thing — forced to offer the same service at the same price.

There's no need to say it, Father. I know it. It's not proper to have such thoughts. Not today. It was bad value, no competition, a rip-off. But sometimes, when I am alone at night, my mind travels back to that glorious prelapsarian time, before we were given free will, free choice and quite so many options. The time before Eve bit into the apple for the *second* time, only to be asked by Adam: 'But are you sure Red Delicious really offers the best value of all the varieties on offer?'

Sixty is the new fifty

Sixty is the new fifty, the baby boomers say; and eighty will soon be the new seventy. I just hope the boomers will manage to redefine death by the time I get there. Maybe 'death' could be the new 'I'm-a-bit-tired'. In the meantime, I'd like forty-six to be the new thirty-three, but somehow it doesn't have the same ring.

In the bush, people are more practical. One friend is turning sixty, and is taking to retirement with rather too much relish. She's just bought a particularly stout pair of shoes which, she eagerly tells everyone, with proper care will 'see me out'. Every purchase is now accompanied by this dour calculation. 'I bought a good one,' she says of her new fridge, 'since that way it will see me out.' She has recently bought her 'last' car, 'last' winter gloves and even her 'last' pair of jeans.

Friends try to jolly her along and suggest that she should be able to go through at least five more pairs of shoes before she pegs out, particularly if she foregoes the proper care and forgets to apply the polish. But she seems to find these suggestions troubling, as if we were impugning her purchasing skill rather than praising her good health.

Perhaps the answer is to buy shoddy goods, just to make yourself feel younger. Shopping at Target, I purchase a particularly cheap electric kettle and a pair of really tacky sandshoes, already falling apart. If I treat both badly, I could go through quite a number of them before I trot off. 'It's my nineteenth last electric kettle,' I will be able to tell the young man on the checkout.

Meanwhile, the government is not interested in such calculations. In the government's view there's just too much malingering going on. Retired people putting their feet up at sixty or sixty-five. Young people avoiding work right up until age fourteen or fifteen. Middle-aged people maintaining only two or three jobs, plus child-care responsibilities. How, the government wonders, do they fill all their spare time?

Everywhere the Treasurer looks he sees people slacking off. Take, for example, the thousands of babies living in Australia. All seem to expect services from the government and yet they contribute nothing in tax. Indeed, many seem to have no other ambition than to lie about and suck on the teat. I say they need to learn to stand on their own two feet. And, a little later, to get on their bikes. Or at least their trikes. Then there are the disabled pensioners, lying around dependent on the taxpayer just because they happen to be missing the odd leg. Well, that's hardly a reason they can't hop to it and stand on their own foot.

Worse still are those Australians who are near death. It's their selfishness that most annoys economists. Some have failed to even dig their own grave at the cemetery. Ask them who'll carry their coffin and it's always: 'Oh, somebody else will do it.' Well, it's not good enough. Not in these times of demographic change.

No wonder the Treasurer wants a revolution in our attitude to work. If there's a single inspiring image of this new world, it's this: a disabled pensioner with only one leg, hopping through the graveyard with a shovel over his arthritic shoulder, moaning quietly due to his chronic emphysema. He finds the right spot and manfully digs his own grave. Only once he's spooned out the last handful of dirt and arranged the roses on the graveside does he finally succumb to illness and exhaustion, tumbling neatly forward into his own grave: stone, cold dead.

Of course, he'll still be *bludging* on someone else to throw the dirt in on top of him . . . but at least he's doing a little to protect the country from the ravages of demographic change.

Once a person is deceased, a lot of people might say: 'Fair enough. He's worked hard — time for a rest.' But here's the point: do the dead have the right to lie there, sponging off the rest of us, just because they've passed into some other 'special category'?

Given the demographic challenges we face, that may be a luxury we just can't afford. Consider the buoyant stone-fruit industry in the Riverina and its urgent need for more scarecrows. It's perfect work for a dead person — not too arduous and yet still a real contribution to our booming economy. It also doesn't need to be full time — just a few days a week will do. The government is not without compassion: the Treasurer understands that once a person is dead he may wish to take things a little easier.

Of course, all these calculations change once you start listening to the longevity experts. Several of them, with an air of quiet confidence, now claim that humans will soon live to the age of 300 — an idea that leaves the Treasurer rubbing his hands together with glee.

Admittedly, if we all live to 300, everything will have to change. At the moment, a twenty-first birthday party comes about a quarter-way through life; under the new system, we'll have to hold it at age seventy-five. The gatecrashers, as usual, will be slightly older than the birthday boy or girl — a rampaging group of thrill-seekers in their mid-eighties, with a taste for rum, Mylanta and mischief. Meanwhile, the midlife crisis will be put off until age 150, with hoards of sesquicentenarians driving sports cars, attempting skydiving and making crazy career shifts. Half Australia's dislocated hips will come from bungee-jumping 180-year-olds.

Age 100 will no more deserve a telegram from the Queen than age thirty-three does right now, and children will live at home until they are at least 120. ('Clean up your room, Batboy. I'm sick of coming in here and finding your dentures on the floor.') It will also be hard to exert parental authority when you are aged 290, and they're just behind at 270. ('I think I'm old enough, Dad, after nearly three centuries, to come home when I damn well want.')

That's why we'll have to make some changes. Age sixteen will be far too young for your first kiss. You'll want to remember that delicious moment for ever, so safer to put it off to age sixty and give your memory an even chance. Losing your virginity should be put off until at least age seventy. That way you can play the field for a good decade, before settling down with that someone special for the next two centuries. The first kneetrembler can happen when you're ninety, by which time your knees will be trembling of their own accord.

The first century of your new marriage may well be the toughest. After a time, you may experience the seventy-year-itch and want to play the field once more. Who could blame you? You're only 170 and have just been fitted with your third set of new hips. Naturally, you'll want to test them out.

But how are our bodies going to cope? Already mine is like a map of past accidents and errors of judgement. Through careful prodding, I can still locate the outline of a Mars Bar I thoughtlessly consumed in 1992. A close inspection of my cheeks shows the pinkish bloom of too much Australian shiraz. I have three deep scars on my thigh from a sporting accident when I was twelve, and a dodgy knee from a misguided attempt at ballet a few years later.

Here's my point: had I known I'd have to make the vehicle last another couple of centuries I may have been more careful.

There are other problems. Your music collection will be spread over twenty-seven different formats, of which LPs, CDs and iPods will only be the first. Hollywood, always keen to push the age difference as far as possible, will feature love affairs between various ingénues and Harrison Ford, who, at this point, will be 280 years old. The Rolling Stones will be playing at the Enmore Theatre in the year 2254. On the roads, the majority of drivers will be over ninety, and the law will be forced to bow to majority opinion. All motorists will be required to wear a hat and have their left indicator blinking permanently.

Back at home, I wash Jocasta's cereal bowl with an angry flourish. I hate the way she just slings it in there. I was going to let it ride, but not with another 260 years of life to go. If I start my campaign now, she may well reform before we're much over 190.

Apparently, it's the new forty.

With a thong in my heart

In the United States District Court
SwimStyle Imports of the USA vs Koala Rubber
of Australia
Judge James Stubbs presiding

Opening statement of Mr Tom Smith, attorney for SwimStyle Imports: My client, a swimwear company headquartered in southern California, pursuant to the objectives of the Free Trade Agreement (FTA) with Australia, did order 20,000 items of a product described as 'a pair of black rubber thongs'. The meaning of the word 'thong' is very clear within this jurisdiction. As Your Honour would be aware, it refers to piece of scanty clothing, by way of a G-string and/or other item of revealing swimwear. The fact that these were offered in black rubber, and as part of a two-for-one deal, only added to their allure in the view of the SwimStyle marketing team.

SwimStyle Imports did not see the necessity of checking the product carefully, as it came from a reputable supplier and under the umbrella of the FTA. The thongs were thus received and immediately packaged as lingerie/bikini wear and supplied into the Californian market. Your Honour would be aware of the situation which followed, with thousands of Californian women walking in public — on beaches and boardwalks — clothed in nothing but an item of Australian rubber footwear, which they wore grasped between their upper thighs.

Certainly, the thick rubber sole cut into their legs; and the waddling gait necessary to keep the thong in place caused several back injures. Many women also discovered it was impossible to sit down without the thong dropping to the floor, with a consequent loss of modesty.

And yet Americans are 'can-do' people. Given the product was labelled as bikini wear, many women were convinced it was simply the new style — albeit one that was particularly revealing, especially when viewed from above. They were determined to find a way it could be worn with comfort.

It was for this reason that many women tried to heat the thong, believing the thick sole could be bent into a more modest shape, thus providing a little more coverage. Sadly, as has been widely reported, once put in position and heated, the rubber has a tendency to melt. While your honour will appreciate the popularity of the Brazilian wax among Californian beach-goers, there are, in our humble submission, less painful ways to achieve one.

Your honour, I note the submission of Koala Rubber on this point. It says, firstly, that the product was never designed to be heated. And that, secondly, the rubber straps provide a sort of handle with which one can pull the thong free of its entanglements.

It is our submission, Your Honour, that the rubber handles merely led to further injuries. Many women, with the heated thong stuck firmly in place, requested assistance from a husband or other male friend. Typically the male helper would prop the woman up in a chair and begin to exert pressure using the rubber straps or, as they saw them, handles. Typically the rubber would begin to stretch while the melted thong was immovable. Your Honour will be aware of the male desire to be successful when offering assistance in this way. Some men recruited friends, and one would often find a whole conga line of helpers heaving on the fixed object, the rubber straps expanding and expanding and expanding, much like a rubber band or slingshot, the woman braced against a low wall or other anchorage point.

The force built up was, of course, incredible, especially when released by the sudden pulling free of the rubber straps. Whole groups of men would be sent sprawling backwards at enormous speed, the thong still immovable. Given the nature of Californian coastal landscape there were, in many cases, cliffs involved.

The 143 cases of death that have followed, together with the seventy-three cases of back pain, 347 cases of involuntary Brazilian waxing, and thousands of cases of inadvertent nudity, have left SwimStyle the subject of legal actions totalling $7.3 billion dollars. We hereby seek leave to countersue the Australian Government for its failure to harmonise Australian language with that used in the rest of the American empire.

Your Honour may ask whether we attempted to settle this matter outside the court system. The answer is a definite yes. As soon as the issue became apparent, SwimStyle's managing director, Mr Denis Kazan, put through a call to the Sydney headquarters of Koala Rubber, speaking to Koala's CEO, Mr Barry Brown. Early in the conversation, Mr Kazan confided that SwimStyle's entire marketing staff were 'all pretty pissed' — a phrase which, within this jurisdiction, is properly taken to convey feelings of anger and disappointment. The response from Mr Brown — which was to guffaw and say 'Well, you all better sober up a little' — leads us to claim supplementary damages of a further $1 billion.

Total damages, Your Honour, amount to the sum of $8.3 billion. We also respectively submit that the FTA be henceforth scrapped until the two countries can at least agree to speak a common language.

Pigsty

I'm sick of these aspirational TV shows in which good-looking hosts in a fever of activity fix up backyards and renovate houses, covering every surface with a rag-rolled finish and every fenceline with a box hedge. Meanwhile, sitting on the couch, you watch as your own house collapses around you. Who needs TV that makes you feel inferior? What about a new show called *Pigsty*? 'We take a beautiful new home — and in twenty-four hours make it look like your place.'

I have tried renovation. I have even attempted 'house-proud'. It doesn't work. Frankly, you're better off wallowing in your own filth. Here's why:

1. The fancier the finish, the less well it lasts. Why do you think past generations of Australians painted everything in mission brown? Not the most attractive of colours but — cunningly — it *starts out* as the

colour you get after thirty years of handling. Now, that's foresight.

2. The more piss-elegant the kitchen benchtop, the more cleaning involved. The previous generation of Australians had a depression to get through, then a war to fight. That's why, en masse, they installed Laminex's 'Baby Chuck' — a subtle combination of grey swirls and tan smudges designed to hide the most slapdash of wipe-downs. *Pigsty*'s advice: hang onto it. (Visit our website: www.just-do-nothing.com)

3. Why the vicious attack on the Hills hoist, traditionally planted dead centre of the backyard? On these shows they are constantly ripping them out — a ritual cutting-down of a past army of Australian men and their contribution to the nation's laundry. Thank God the old buggers have had their revenge: installing each hoist in such a huge ball of cement that generations of younger men have done in their backs shifting them.

4. On these shows they ring a tradesman and then, a few hours later, he shows up, clean, tidy, on time and ready to work. So how come they call it 'reality TV'?

5. What's the story with 'opening up the house to the backyard'? That means you can *see* the backyard. That means you've got to *fix up* the backyard. That means you can't leave it permanently littered with toys, bikes, engine blocks and part-built cubbies.

6. Why the obsession with 'opening up the kitchen to the dining room'? That means you can *see* the dinner guests. It also means they can see you and what you are doing to their food. Overall point: what do these people have against walls?

7. On all these TV shows, renovations are achieved in twenty-four hours. In reality they take months. One friend of mine drew the line when, getting up at midnight to breastfeed her twins, she found two neighbourhood dogs fornicating in her lounge room. She blamed this on her husband who had removed the side wall of their home some months before and hadn't *quite* got around to rebuilding it. I don't believe he's done any DIY since. Or had much opportunity to produce more twins.

8. Why does every door have to be a sliding one? On these shows they love them. Have they shares in the ball-bearing business? And do they realise all sliding doors fall to pieces after five years, usually taking the marriage with them?

9. Why, in shows like *Backyard Blitz* or *Renovation Rescue*, do they have to install at least three different materials underfoot — a little paving, an area of loose stones and some pressed elephant dung to 'reflect the owner's continuing fascination with Africa'? Whatever happened to the notion of concreting the bastard over then painting it green? As in the phrase 'he came, he saw, he concreted'.

10. Fashion changes every decade. No sooner will you have levered out the aluminium windows and replaced them with timber than the host will be on screen: 'Have you considered installing aluminium windows? They're the latest "must-have".'

11. The end is never in sight. You imagine in five years time you'll be able to rest on your laurels. Or rather, rest on your delightfully modish wicker chairs atop

your new tallow-wood deck. Wrong! A more accurate analogy is the painting of the Sydney Harbour Bridge — by the time you've painted your way to one end, the other end will already be peeling and rusting. Easier, really, to do nothing.

12. Any attempt to copy the renovations achieved on the TV will fail anyway, since your tools are not up to the job. I know the modern man is mocked for always blaming his tools; he is compared unfavourably to old Uncle Frank who could achieve anything around the house minutes after the problem was identified. 'All Auntie Vera had to do was point out the problem.' Yes, I know. But consider the riches of Uncle Frank's resources. The man had a shed. With power. The shed had a fridge. He had copies of *Australasian Post* in there. And his own body weight in high-class chisels. I — we — have the hall cupboard, down the back of which, once you've moved the vacuum cleaner to one side and displaced the baby bath, just in case we have another child, which by the way we're not going to, you'll find a sad and tangled pile of cheap tools, mostly purchased from the bargain bin outside Clint's Crazy Bargains. There are chisels that, for want of anything better, you've attempted to use as screwdrivers. There are set squares that you've used as paint-tin openers. There's a socket set that you once pressed into service as a hammer. Now, if we only had better tools . . .

13. And, finally, whatever they say in these shows, it is impossible to make a house look better through painting or renovating. The lovely job you've done on

the bedroom walls only serves to draw attention to your battered old wardrobe and threadbare carpet. Last week, they looked fine; now they dominate the room — as visible as a pimple on a fashion model's chin. You spend more money, purchase new carpet and wardrobes, and the bedrooms look perfect. Which only serves to draw attention to the hallway, which used to look fine, but now . . .

Well, that's all from the team at Pigsty *for another week. We'll be back with more will-sapping and life-defeating advice next week.*

Not drowning, waiving

Welcome to life. I note that you are a baby, recently born. While your auditory and intellectual processes may not be completely developed, it is nonetheless my duty to present to you certain disclaimers and warranty waivers. Please stop sucking that blanket and listen.

Life in Australia may contain traces of nuts. In fact, there are nuts everywhere. Especially in the legal system. That's just my little joke. Are you sure you don't want to take notes? I shall make an annotation that you waived that constitutional right. Your gurgle shall be taken as a note of assent.

Swim between the flags. Don't get involved in schoolyard fights. Check the pavement ahead as you walk. Don't smoke in bed. And don't sit naked on a chair with moving parts. Actually, that one is mainly for the boy babies, but you never know. Also: all hot liquids in Australia may prove to be, well, hot. And before you dive into water, please check the depth.

There's no need to look at me like that. These days, we have to place warnings on everything, so it's easier to do them in one go. Straight after birth, which is what I'm doing right now. Dry-clean everything. Or at least hand-wash. Can I be very clear about that? And please stop sucking that blanket. It may have traces of nuts.

Never eat a meal bigger than your own head. Do not attempt to wash the bottom of your feet in the shower while drunk. And never go fly-fishing while wearing a nose ring. People do, you know. And then they sue State Recreation for providing the river in which they were fly-fishing. It's been most lamentable. But you won't be able to sue, Baby Number 4305789. You've heard the official warning.

What else? Always check for ceiling fans before jumping for joy. If working in the building trade, always get someone else to carry the bag of cement. And don't try to queue jump in the delicatessen if there are elderly Italian women ahead of you in the queue. Oh, yes, the injuries can be horrific. But the warning has now been given. No suing the Department of Multicultural Affairs for you.

I really would like you to stop sucking that blanket. While the sucking is occurring in front of me — a government official — that fact should in no way be implied as an endorsement of your actions. That is a state hospital blanket. God knows where it has been. I wouldn't suck it. I think you're crazy. But it's your choice. The risk has been disclosed and thus accepted.

What else? Never argue with bouncers. If you find yourself in a restaurant that is revolving, you've probably had too much to drink. And before commencing an uncharitable anecdote about a person, always check that the subject of the anecdote is not among those listening.

I could go on, and in fact I will: Don't wear platform shoes when attempting the Macarena. Roof racks, men and octopus straps make a very unhappy combination. When fixing a gun, don't stare down the barrel when trying to assess why nothing is coming out when you pull the trigger. And once you turn sixteen, you may wish to store certain unctions and potions in your bedside drawers so they can be readily located in the dark. But do find a different drawer for the Dencorub.

Will you stop fidgeting? We're nearly there. Never place a rose between your teeth without first removing the thorns. Don't wear hoop earrings while operating heavy machinery. And never put anything smaller than your elbow into your ear. I know that's what your grandmother told you but when I say it, it has legal weight. I'm recording this you know. What else? Get an electrician. Get an electrician. Get an electrician.

You'll find another 5300 warnings in this pamphlet, which I am conveying to you by the act of putting it inside your cot. Don't suck it. It may contain nuts.

The Cupboard

One of the mysteries of holidays is the way we drive hundreds of kilometres in order to stay somewhere less comfortable than home. Maybe it's our way of consoling ourselves about the year ahead: sure, we'll have to go back to work, but at least we'll get to move back into our normal home.

Until then, it's a week up the coast with the scratched plastic wine tumblers, the broken banana lounge for which we'll probably get the blame, the windows with the ripped flywire, and a hot water supply that's defeated by one shower and a bit of washing up.

Why is it so? Why are all rental houses up the coast the same?

How come they never supply a big pot in which you can boil pasta? Is it a state government rule? 'There can only be three saucepans — each one smaller than the last.' Is there a decree that, during all official holidays, the whole population must boil pasta in batches, in tiny saucepans, on whatever hotplates they can goad into life?

Which brings us to the hotplates. Why is it that the back left one never works? It's like a rule of nature. By what strange practice do they become damaged? Do people leap up and down on them? Or is it some sort of agreement among the estate agents? ('Oh no, son, you can't offer a fully working stove. Next thing you know, they'll all be wanting one.') And where do they purchase these special electric frypans — the ones that burn a crop-circle into the food by means of a red-hot element which leaves the rest of the pan dead cold?

The TV set, I must admit, generally works, although the remote control is long lost, requiring you to prod at various tiny buttons in the machine's tummy. I say it's lost, but more likely it's in The Cupboard — the locked shrine at the heart of any beach rental property.

This is the place in which The Owners put all The Good Stuff, so The Renters can't wreck it. God knows what is in there, but as a renter it's always the first thing you spot: the locked cupboard, or occasionally the locked garage. You stare at it, your imagination running wild.

Presumably it's like Ali Baba's cave in there — crowded with all the things that would make the house *perfect*. Ah, yes, there'd be pasta pots aplenty, piled high, jostling for position with a DVD player, a real teapot, an egg slide without a burnt and melted handle, and some curtains that would actually keep out the sun in the morning.

In various houses, I have sat in the baking heat of the late afternoon — a sheen of sweat on my forehead, panting lightly from heat sickness — wondering why, in a house this hot, there are no fans. But, of course, there are plenty of fans: it's just that they are all locked up in Ali Baba's Cupboard.

I imagine the owner collecting them, just before he leaves, cackling as he stacks them in The Cupboard: 'This will stop them using up my electricity; let them sweat it out.' I imagine him rather like Gollum in *The Lord of the Rings* — his eyes ablaze as he lifts the Electrolux 240-volt RC-17 Turbo Fan into The Cupboard. 'Ah, my precious,' he says, stroking it lasciviously, 'you rest until my return.'

Last year things got so hot in our fanless rental, we spent a couple of afternoons at the local Bi-Lo supermarket — playing cards on the benches near the checkout. The airconditioning was wonderful, although there's nothing like another price check in aisle three to make you forget you're in possession of the joker.

While at Bi-Lo, of course, we could stock up on the chemicals required to keep at bay Australia's wonderful and diverse wildlife. The real estate agent may have advertised the house as 'sleeps eight', but that's not including the permanent occupants: about 5000 sandflies; a dozen battalions of mosquitos; a heaving mass of cockroaches; and some insane kookaburras with psycho-killer eyes.

With our chemical ammunition from Bi-Lo, each evening is like a scene from *Survivor* — the tribal council scene — as we try to eat our meal outside, surrounded by burning plumes of citronella, our legs wet and stinging with Aerogard, a stick at the ready to hold at bay the meat-hungry kookaburras.

How does the owner cope? How does he stand it? My eyes again flick to The Cupboard. What's he got in there? He must have something *really* good: a secret stash of the hard stuff — smoke bombs and mozzie zappers; litres of banned DDT; spray packs full of agent orange, sitting in rusted tins, saved up from the Vietnam War.

I imagine him up here — luxuriating on his mozzie-free balcony, pasta bubbling away in its large pot, an episode of *Seinfeld* twinkling away on the DVD, as the door to The Cupboard swings idly open in the breeze created by the massed banks of fans.

Anyone know how to pick a lock?

The little read books

The film industry is always attacked for doing the same thing over and over again; but not the book industry. Every year the booksellers' catalogues contain ideas that are just so fresh and original. Why not take a look at this year's bumper crop?

Whoops! Some Poo Just Came out of My Bum by I.P. Nightly. Another scatological triumph from the international author. Why not buy the set, including the sequels *Whoops! Some Poo Came Out of My Bum Again*, and *Whoops! Some Poo Came Out of My Dog's Bum*. Who but I.P. Nightly could reveal that children find poo and wee jokes this funny? Guaranteed to give children a lifelong love of reading — but only of poo and wee jokes.

How Come Everyone Else Isn't as Spiritual as Me? by Michael Lunatic. Yet another volume in a lifelong series by the Melbourne poet and cartoonist, in which he points out that that ordinary people lead lives of mediocrity and desolation due to their strange unwillingness to be more like Michael Lunatic. Volume forty-three in the series.

How I Took Off My Fancy Pants by **Catherine d'Oats**. Prose like this has been found for decades in dirty magazines such as *Penthouse* and *Hustler*. Yet Catherine d'Oats is a French intellectual, a female and a dead-set fancy-pants type writer. No wonder this work has sold 300,000 copies and been hailed as a breakthrough in our understanding of human desire. Maybe what's special is knowing that Catherine has such a large vocabulary yet chooses to use only those words that have four letters. (Claims that Catherine d'Oats is the *nom de plume* of a bloke called Barry who runs a London chain of dirty cinemas are currently the subject of legal action.)

Grind! by **Professor Joseph Brezenski**. Last year it was the history of the screwdriver; before that the history of the clock, the zipper and the salted cod. Now Harvard historian Joseph Brezenski has spent ten years charting the history of the pepper grinder. As he puts it: 'Through studying this one artefact, the whole history of human civilisation can be told — from the first journeys into the new world, through to the development of the very large pepper grinder in today's Italian restaurants.' Certainly the professor's thrilling narrative of innovation and revolution, set against the conservative world of the spice establishment, is well worth its 670 pages. The professor is currently working on a history of the sock, in two companion volumes, one on the history of the right sock, and one on the history of the left.

Boo Hoo. It Wasn't My Fault. An Anthology of Australian Political Memoirs. Collected in one volume, here are the political memoirs of a whole generation of Australian politicians — divided up according to their excuse for why it all went belly-up. With an introduction by British TV star Ali G, chapters include: Is It Because I Black?; Is It Because I Woman?; and Is It Because I Just a Deadhead?

***The Buttered Toast Book* by Jamie Olive.** Who needs to buy a single cookbook when you can fill your house with specialist volumes — whole thumping tomes dedicated to oysters, eggs or artichokes? In this beautifully designed book, Jamie Olive tells you how to make toast — including advice on how to choose the freshest bread at the supermarket; how to spread the butter right to the edges; plus a sumptuous photo display of jams and marmalades. And here's the good news: at $97.50 you'll have no money left for anything other than toast. Jamie's companion volume, *The Water Book — How to Pour It, How to Taste It and How to Enjoy it with Friends*, will be out in the autumn.

***Pulling Up Stumps* by Wayne Warrens.** Cricket books are not actually meant to be read; they are meant to be given — usually to an elderly uncle who'll receive the gift by mumbling miserably: 'I don't know why she gave me a book. I've already got a book.' This one has a durable cover and a cheap price, and so comes Highly Recommended.

***White Knuckles* by Zadie Zee.** Being a writer used to be one of the few artistic jobs in which you could achieve fame and fortune without being good-looking. Thank goodness that loophole has finally been closed. Evelyn Waugh, George Orwell and H.G. Wells — all of them just too ugly to make it in today's British literary scene. Sure Zadie Zee's prose is unremarkable and her stories poorly developed, but check out the author picture on the back! Alas, Hanif Kureishi and Margaret Atwood write better books, but compare the author shots. No wonder bookshops have now made it compulsory to purchase Zadie's novel by the time-honoured method of not stocking anything else.

Happy reading.

defeated

'Our income is zero. The salary goes into the bank but it's spoken for before it lands. It's like throwing a dead dog into a tank of piranhas. Gone within minutes. Just a few scraps floating to the surface. Going to the Flexiteller is like being witness to a massacre. Can we move onto the next question, if you don't mind?'

Count me out

It's census night and Sally Smith-Frazzle is at home, ready to fill out the official form. But she finds it's impossible to give yes/no answers to all these questions. Maybe she'll just have to bail up the census collector and explain first-hand some of the complexities of life.

'Well, what's your name?' asks the census collector.

'It's Frazzle. Well, actually it's Smith-Frazzle. We hyphenated to suit the kids but when Becky started high school she got embarrassed, so we stick with Frazzle now, except for the older boy, who hates his father so much he refuses to use the name. I take the piss out of him and call him The Boy Formerly Known as Frazzle but he just gives me a hostile stare. As if it's my fault that Trevor's his father. I tell him: "Why blame me? Blame the overproof Bundy rum at the Willow Hotel in Fremantle." But it's hard to get through to teenagers, don't you reckon?'

'The next thing is income,' says the census collector. 'You need to write in your income.'

'In what sense do you mean income? In the sense that money comes in and Trevor and I sit down and decide how to spend it? You've got to be joking. Put down zero. Our income is zero. The salary goes into the bank but it's spoken for before it lands. It's like throwing a dead dog into a tank of piranhas. Gone within minutes. Just a few scraps floating to the surface. Going to the Flexiteller is like being witness to a massacre. Can we move onto the next question, if you don't mind?'

'Your age?'

'Based on date of birth? Or how we look in the mirror? And if it's the mirror, are you talking morning or night? Take a reading before breakfast and you'd be handing me a senior's card. Here's the problem: I was one of those people that went straight from pimples to wrinkles. I was aged thirty-five years, three months and seven days — and then the changeover hit. Squeezed my last pimple on Monday. By Wednesday I looked like a geriatric bloodhound. I just regret I didn't have more fun on the Tuesday night. It was like *Anne of the Thousand Days*. I had a window of opportunity of about three hours. I could have worked my way through the front bar of the Manzil Room and then spent the next ten years resting up. But you don't know these things at the time, do you?'

'Gender?'

'We certainly started out as man and woman. I remember that quite clearly. But it gets a bit harder to tell once you hit your forties. Trevor's now drinking so much beer I swear he's started to develop breasts. About a B-cup, I'd say. Quite perky, not too saggy. Put some tassels on them and you'd have quite a show. I half suspect he's slowly turning into a woman. Catch him side-on and you'd say he was pregnant. About eight months, with the baby lying breach. Sometimes I look at him sitting on the couch, and I say to myself, "That man could go into first stage labour at any moment and here I am just lying around. I should be plotting the fastest route to the hospital."

'Not that he's the only one experiencing a sex change. I seem to be slowly turning into a bloke. Every week Trevor loses more hair off his body and somehow it's popping up on mine. It's like some weird transference is going on. I've tried sleeping with a pillow between us but still it happens. Once you're down past my hips, it's like *The Planet of the Apes*. Actually, you look a bit that way yourself; maybe we could share some tips for keeping it at bay?'

'What about this question? Number in household tonight? Do you think you can manage that?'

'Depends what we are eating. The boy likes meat. Promise him meat and he'll be here. Otherwise it's YMCA — Yesterday's Muck Cooked Again. Tonight? Trevor's cooking tonight — chops, sausages and a bit of bacon. The boy calls it Turf and Turf. I've promised to make Bad-for-you-potatoes. It's my signature dish. Spuds with about half a ton of dairy product. Without it, Trevor would be half the man he is today. I could give you like the recipe, if you'd like.'

'Do you speak a language other than English at home?'

'I'd have to say yes. The Boy Formerly Known as Frazzle doesn't really speak at all. He just grunts. Who knows what language he's trying to speak, but it's certainly not English. Trevor and I used to talk our heads off but you run out of steam after a while. We still communicate through body language. You might like to write that down: the language of love. Even with the breasts, he's still a very attractive man. Maybe even more attractive. Now, will that be all?'

The teenage boys' guide to water conservation

Life is so confusing. As a teenage boy I conserved water with the best of them. I never showered; cleaned my teeth only occasionally; didn't need to shave; forgot to flush; and left all the dirty plates in the sink 'for Later'. I also failed to water pot plants, even ones left in my direct care, with the result that they died, never to require a drop of water again.

In retrospect: I was a water crusader; an environmental saint. If the fifteen-year-old me was around right now, the green movement would give me a medal. What others called 'grubby', 'skanky' and 'downright stomach-turning' was merely a zealous attitude to water conservation. With Australia now facing a water crisis, I look back over the conversations I've had with various flatmates over the years and find in them a veritable How-to Guide to Water Savings.

1. **Clothes don't need to be washed; they merely need to be rested.** Again, the young men of Australia have long had the right idea. For a start, you should never take off clothes and fold them or hang them up in the wardrobe. Instead, spread them in a thin layer all over your bedroom floor, as you might cover a back lawn with top soil. (Tip: to get an even spread, simply let the clothes drop wherever you happen to take them off.) Certainly, the bedroom will soon be enveloped in fumes, but these fumes represent the cleaning process in action. The odours prove that dirt is *leaving* the clothes and *entering* the air. You can figure out the science: the more fumes, the more cleaning action you have going on. At the end of a couple of weeks, pick up the T-shirt nearest to you, pop it on and think of the water you've saved.

2. **Place a brick in the toilet cistern.** After a while you'll realise this means you have to flush two, three or four times after every use so pitiful is the amount of water now in the cistern. Your water bills will be huge. At this point, remove the brick from the cistern and pop it inside the toilet bowl itself. The sight of a large red house-brick inside your toilet will put off most people, and suddenly your water bill will shrink.

3. **Don't shower with a friend.** Such showers can go for hours. Communal showering was one of the reasons the sixties revolution petered out; that along with self-destructive drug use, self-referential politics and nits. My advice: shower with an enemy. The more the two of you hate each other, the quicker will be your showers. An ex-wife or -husband will do fine; or try

the idiot business partner who sent you both
bankrupt.

4. **Consider purchasing a waterless toilet.** Many
    people are choosing the new microwave toilets. One
    problem: once you've seen what a microwave does to
    popcorn you may want to keep your pants on in its
    presence.

5. **Don't wash the plates**. It is extremely wasteful to
    wash plates and pots as you go; far better to leave for
    Later — as young men tend to call their female
    flatmates. She'll be able to do a whole week's worth
    in one go. It's a great feeling, incidentally, when you
    first sling the pots and plates into the sink, knowing
    you're doing your bit for the environment.

6. **Ditto cleaning the toilet.** Leave it for Later. Remember,
    it's not called the Patriarchal Cistern for nothing.
    Another point: if the manufacturer expected them to be
    cleaned, would they bother fitting them with a lid?

7. **The shower recess does not need cleaning.** Not by
    you, her or anyone else. The principle is simple
    enough: every time you have a shower, the shower
    has a shower. There's hot water, there's solvents,
    there's occasionally singing; if that's not 'cleaning the
    shower recess' I don't know what is. For those who
    use yet more water to give the shower its own
    personal shower, I say shame on you: think of the
    damn dam.

8. **If something does, by accident, get washed, never
    use a steam iron to press it.** Just place it between
    your mattress and bed-base and sleep on it for a few
    weeks.

9. **Ban wet T-shirt competitions.** Not only are they sexist, they are also wasteful of water. In the spirit of water conservation, far better for the T-shirt to be simply removed.

10. **Stop criticising young guys.** All our lives people have criticised us. Visiting girlfriends. The occasional tidy male. Mothers. Real estate agents. Council rat catchers. All of them would make plain their feelings. They would criticise and complain. Oh, that we knew then what we know now. 'Steady on, maaaaate,' we'd have said. 'I'm just trying to save water.'

It certainly is difficult being ahead of one's time.

Vision statement

For six months, every breakfast has been a misery. 'You need glasses,' Jocasta says matter-of-factly, as she spoons down her cereal. 'Go on admit it. It's just vanity that's stopping you. You just can't admit you're getting old.'

'I don't need glasses,' I reply with measured dignity, as I resume my reading of the newspaper. 'I just find the printer's ink a little smelly at this time of day. That's why I choose to hold the newspaper at arm's length.'

Jocasta was issued with her reading glasses six months ago. To be ahead of her partner in this matter has been driving her crazy. As soon as we sit down to read the paper it begins. 'The way you're holding that paper is ridiculous,' she'll announce, peering at me over the top of her new glasses. 'Is there any way you could be holding it further away? I mean, give it six months and you'll need a pair of binoculars just to get the gist of the TV guide. Two years on and you'll need the Hubble Telescope.'

I ignore these attacks but secretly realise something is amiss. The newspaper, I come to understand, is in the grip of drastic cost-cutting — with stealthy reductions in the type size just to save money. It is a scandal not limited to the newspaper industry; I spot the same practice among the major book publishers, and noticeably among the manufacturers of supermarket goods. On cans, pill packets and cereal boxes the information on the back is now impossible to read.

In the face of this conspiracy I have no choice but to approach Jocasta's optometrist and seek assistance. I arrive at the shopping mall with the name and address Jocasta has supplied. I'm surprised to discover that the optometrist is a disturbingly young man with no apparent need to wear spectacles himself.

He takes me into his rooms. It's quite a process. Once in the chair, the young man swings this huge metal contraption in front of my eyes. It has two tiny eyeholes surrounded by metal levels and multicoloured cogs: it's like being fitted with a pair of Elton John's sunglasses. He asks me to read off various charts.

'It's all part of the ageing process,' he says, as he twiddles with Elton's glasses. 'As we age, the muscles in the eyes can weaken,' he continues, using the word 'we' even though he clearly isn't doing much ageing himself. 'You'll find that process may continue as ageing proceeds.'

Frankly, I don't care for his overuse of the term 'ageing'. Nor his wrinkle-free, spectacle-free face which stares down at me. It's like being served a bottle of overproof rum by a teetotaller barman. I wonder if I should write a complaint letter to his employer.

I toy with asking him whether he can look up Jocasta's eye-test results and whisper them to me. That way I could head home and tell Jocasta how far ahead of me she is in the race towards old age, infirmity and bed-wetting. I then remember her first appointment and how she'd come home in such high spirits, describing the optometrist as 'very helpful, quite young and extremely good-looking'. Certainly the complaint letter will be a long one.

'I think you do need a little assistance,' the young man says brightly, sweeping Elton's spare pair to one side. His eyes sparkle with good health, as he jots down a series of numbers on his pad — no doubt optometrists' code for 'silly old goat, blind as a bat: get out the Coke-bottle bottoms and do it quick.'

A week later the new glasses arrive and I pick them up on the way home. Jocasta can't believe her luck.

'Your eyes look huge in them. It's like living with Marty Feldman. Or some sort of hyperthyroid bug.' With that, she rushes towards me. 'Quick, let me have a go,' she says, slipping them on and squealing with delight. 'The prescription must be three, four times as strong as mine. You're so much blinder than me!'

The glasses certainly give me a new angle on the world. Suddenly everything close up is magnified. I stare down at the keyboard as I type and my hands look alarmingly large, like they've suddenly grown by twenty-five per cent. I glance over to the phone on my desk and reel back startled. The thing is twice its normal size, as if it's bulked up on steroids. I feel like Gulliver in the land of giants. I take the glasses off and let them dangle on a string around my neck. I look like a baffled librarian.

'Don't worry about it,' says Jocasta. 'It's true, your pair is stronger than mine but that won't last for ever. I'm feeling the need to go back to that optometrist quite soon, just to have a good look at his charts. That guy, he's a sight for sore eyes.'

I sit down at my keyboard and adjust my spectacles. It's good to have a strong pair when a letter of complaint gets *this* lengthy.

Fat chance

Australia, we're told, is in the grip of an Obesity Epidemic. The problem is so bad the government has even hosted an Obesity Summit, which I think is the wrong name. It makes me think of a group of red-faced fat men sitting atop Kosciusko, panting from the effort of getting there. They'd be better with the Obesity Depression, which might better sum up the nature of the problem.

Mind you, I've been doing my bit to help. A few months ago, I signed up at a gym, paid $400, and now never turn up. Already my wallet is a lot lighter. The downside is they send me perky letters, straight off the word processor, with lots of exclamation marks!! 'Hi Richard!! It's a beautiful day down here at the gym!!! Where are you!!!! We are missing you!!!!!'

This is so stomach-turning I usually bring up my breakfast. Already I am four kilos lighter. The program is worth every cent.

I have some friends in the *posher* suburbs who've gone for the opposite approach. They go to a bloke who shouts at them. Apparently he's a former Hungarian secret policeman. If you break your diet you get the full treatment of terror and torture. I love the idea of rich people paying to be abused. You can imagine how the one-upmanship will develop: 'Our personal trainer was a paid thug at Israel's Mossad headquarters.'

'Darling, that's nothing, our chappie ran the interrogations at South Africa's notorious Modderbee prison. When he says to me "Run, kaffir, run," the weight just pours off me. He's such a bastard, it's divine.'

Lucy will have a paid assassin from Russia; Jilly an ageing Chilean secret policeman; while Ross will be seeing a standover merchant from Chinatown: 'Ross, you either lose the five kilos by Saturday or there won't be an unbroken lobster tank in your whole house.'

I think our local gym is better. It's mixed: men and women; fat and thin. Every time a young woman walks in, all the middle-aged men on exercise bikes pick up speed. It's wonderful to watch. As soon as she's gone, they slow down again, fighting for breath. I wonder if this could be a new source of green energy: whole squads of middle-aged men on bikes wired up to the national grid with an aerobics class starting somewhere nearby. There may be some fatalities but it's a risk we'd be willing to take for the sake of global warming.

Meanwhile, incidental exercise is now all the rage. The experts say you can get big results by making tiny changes. Already I'm watching SBS more, since its position on the remote control makes it a real stretch for my index finger.

And if I switch to Tasmanian beer, I'll have to use an opener each time I reach for a bottle. This, I think, is what experts mean by 'dieting smart'.

I've also developed my own diet called the Mechanical Breakdown Diet. This involves sitting on the couch after you've had dinner. Every ten minutes you jump up, walk to the fridge and conduct a battle of wills while standing bathed in the fridge's ghostly light. Eventually, you master yourself and sit down again, having eaten nothing. The process is repeated all night until the fridge breaks down and you have to throw out all the food, which makes the next day's dieting so much easier.

Sadly, even this method is not entirely successful. Perhaps we need a dieters' code of practice:

1. A second helping of dinner contains no calories, as long as it is eaten directly from the plate of leftovers while standing at the kitchen counter.

2. Squares of cooking chocolate contain no calories, as long as they're eaten straight from the fridge while bathed in the light of the open door.

3. If you eat something but don't really like the taste, then the calories don't count. Feel free to fetch yourself something better.

4. As noted in my book *In Bed with Jocasta*, broken biscuits located at the bottom of the Tupperware contain no calories. (Since publication of the book, I have heard of some people purposely breaking biscuits in order to render them broken. This is, however, not permitted. Even dieters should have *some* standards.)

5.   Fundraising chocolates contain no calories, their consumption better covered by the phrase 'community service' than by the brutally reductive term 'eating'.

6.   If there's only one slice of cake left, its consumption is best described by the phrase 'saving Glad Wrap' than by the mean-hearted observation 'breaking your diet'.

7.   Licking icing from utensils at the end of the cooking process involves no intake of calories.

8.   If the product is labelled 'lite', go ahead and eat twice as much.

9.   Dessert eaten in a restaurant does contain calories — but only if you were the one who placed the order. Feel free to encourage your partner to order dessert while demurring politely: 'Oh no, not for me, I just couldn't. I'm absolutely full.' Once the plate arrives, lean over menacingly with a spare fork and polish off the lot, down to licking the plate with a maniacal laugh and warning off others with your knife.

10.   Celery, bran and spinach all contain negative calories. Eating them in large quantities allows you to double your consumption of everything else.

11.   Ice-cream scraped off the bottom of the lid contains no calories.

12.   Sausages which have fallen off the BBQ contain no calories.

13.   The last piece of cheese on a platter does contain calories but only if eaten in one go. Try cutting it in half, eating that, cutting it in half again, then eating that, and so on until there is just a tiny sliver left. Then eat the sliver on the basis that 'there's only the tiniest sliver left'.

14. Crackling consumed while carving is exempt from calories. So is any food eaten while cooking.

15. A bite taken from your child's chocolate bar contains no calories, as long as the bite is preceded by the explanation: 'I'm just checking it's not poisoned.'

16. Chips from McDonald's contain no calories if eaten from your child's packet and preceded by the explanation: 'I just wanted to check they were hot.'

17. Food cooked by your child is exempt.

18. Birthday cake eaten while standing at a child's birthday party is exempt.

19. Food left over after filling a Tupperware container is fair game, and your actions, standing there at the kitchen counter, are best described by the phrase 'tidying up' than by the overly pointed 'being a disgusting pig'.

20. The quicker you bolt something down, the fewer calories it has. Remember: squares of chocolate only contain calories if you are fully cognisant of what you are doing.

21. You can eat anything — three pies and a box of donuts — providing you wash it down responsibly with a couple of Diet Cokes.

22. If you slice the ham thinly you can have twice as much.

23. Any failure to lose weight is due to one having 'a slow metabolism' or 'big bones'.

24. If your diet is not working, feel free to choose a different diet. Or, even better, different friends. By surrounding yourself with fatter mates, you'll instantly look thinner.

25. And, finally, there is a complete exemption for food eaten after a particularly horrendous day at work. Or, for that matter, a particularly wonderful day. Indeterminate, mediocre, neither-good-nor-bad days can also be pretty hard to take in a way that can only really be redeemed by a good self-saucing butterscotch pudding.

I'm happy to give evidence on all these matters to the Obesity Summit. Just as soon as they install a lift to get me there.

An unsustainable financial proposition

The Neatwhistles are a quiet and industrious family who, up to this week, have rarely been in the news. Yet late yesterday Jenny Neatwhistle felt it necessary to issue a dramatic profit warning for the family group, pointing to rising input costs and 'bugger all' chances of a pay rise. Grocery cost projections, last calculated in January, had not taken account of the growth in appetite of their sons, Mark, Hugo and Philip, who these days 'just pack it away like there's no tomorrow'. In addition, income from Lotto investments had been well down on expectations in the June quarter, with suggestions that Tom Neatwhistle be forced to reconsider his current system of choosing all six numbers from the last but bottom row.

Some analysts say they are surprised the Neatwhistles have been able to limp on this long, and have questioned the income base of the whole operation.

Says Bill Moneypenny, an analyst with the Bank of Texas-BRL Porkbros: 'At least half the group's income is dependent on Tom Neatwhistle and yet he's in his mid-forties, and unlikely to see any real growth in income. Plus, with every year, his running costs rise.' Indeed, says Moneypenny, close study of the family accounts reveals that Tom has taken to buying wine at $14.90 a bottle, telling his wife that 'If a bloke can't have a decent drop when he's over forty, then what's the point of it all?'

Moneypenny says this has broken the 'psychologically important $10 barrier', and could result in an almost limitless blow-out just keeping Tom running. 'You watch,' he says. 'By December it will be the Wynns Cab-Sav at $18 a go and I'm talking weeknights.'

The situation does not improve even when you examine Jenny's contribution to the income stream garnered through work as a teacher in the education sector.

Says Moneypenny: 'The Neatwhistles' sector exposure is all wrong: they're fully weighted in mature low-growth sectors. They also are carrying these three completely unproductive boys.' Moneypenny says the initial decision to have the boys was made in the late 1980s 'when people were making all sorts of mad decisions to expand', but years later they were still splashing nothing but red all over the balance sheet.

'It's hard to see what contribution they will ever make, except the odd pack of smelly soap on Jenny's birthday and some bath gel at Christmas. Having boys is like investing in a boutique winery — OK if you can stand the losses and the constant disappointments.'

During a detailed phone call, Moneypenny questioned Jenny's future plans, suggesting that she get rid of the underperforming parts of the group — Tom and the three boys — and seek some high-value exposure in new areas. Says Moneypenny: 'There's far too much sentimentality in these small family groups. It may be that Tom could achieve a pay rise, yet he's too scared to ask his boss for one. At the same time his health care costs have doubled over the last four years. Does Jenny pay for the back operation that Tom desperately needs or is it just throwing good money after bad? These are the sort of decisions the group faces.'

Tom, however, disputes the analysis. He says that he and three other non-executive directors have been deceived and had no idea of the problems emerging for the group. 'Honestly, we've been kept in the dark,' Tom says. 'I'd also like to ask some questions of this Bill Moneypenny. Frankly, I think he'd like to see the break-up of the group. I question his motives.'

Moneypenny admits that if a break-up of the group did occur, then it would be 'only natural' for him to seek exposure to the group's best performing sectors. 'And, yes, I guess that means Jenny.'

Interviewed in his 43rd-floor office, atop Sydney's imposing Semtex Tower, Moneypenny admits he first met Jenny at university in the late 1970s. He proposed a merger at the time but found himself rebuffed. 'I think I was a bit too pushy, a bit too brash,' admits Moneypenny, 'but today I think I could really offer her something.'

Says Jenny: 'Of course, it's nice to get the overtures from Bill after all these years. He's a real sweetie but Tom and I remain on course. The approach has been useful. It has brought problems out into the open, where the group will be able to address them in the coming period.'

At last night's meeting of stakeholders, Tom's back operation was green-lighted, the three boys agreed to do more work around the house, the blow-out in Tom's drinking was tackled, and a new Lotto strategy was agreed upon, based on filling out the second but top line.

As Jenny puts it: 'I guess there's lots of ways of reading the same balance sheet.'

Decline and fall

Madonna, the American singer, has revealed she's a different mother with her second child than with her first — less paranoid and more relaxed. She's not the first parent to notice how attitudes shift with each additional child.

First child: 'We've decided to play Beethoven sonatas to him while he's in the womb and read him passages from the great poets.'

Second child: 'Whenever there's classical music on a TV ad I turn it up.'

Third child: 'I'm sick of the little bugger kicking me. It's not my fault *Big Brother* is over.'

First child: 'He's only two days old and he just gave me a smile. I think he's advanced.'

Second child: 'When he burps it almost looks like a smile — so cute.'

Third child: 'He's the farting champion of the Western World. At least there's now no doubt who the father is.'

First child: 'We've repainted the room and I've hand-stencilled some animal pictures onto the ceiling.'

Second child: 'There's a room off the back that's not too bad, and when he's older we'll move all the boxes.'

Third child: 'Kick the dog out and there's a perfectly good spot there by the back door.'

First child: 'He's got fourteen different hand-knitted cardigans and ten pairs of OshKosh pilchers.'

Second child: 'Target had twenty per cent off, so we bought a job lot.'

Third child: 'If we soak the jumpsuits long enough, you'll hardly notice the stains and silverfish holes.'

First child: 'We've booked him into four different schools, started an investment scheme and put him on the waiting list for the Melbourne Club.'

Second child: 'Nana's opened an account at the Commonwealth Bank and whacked in the first five dollars.'

Third child: 'I just wish someone could come up with a name. When he starts high school he's going to hate being called Bub.'

First child: 'I don't think he knows what a lolly is. I don't allow them in the house.'

Second child: 'We're trying to keep a limit on it, especially on weekdays.'

Third child: 'Quick, your Dad's in the shower. Let's split the pack of Tim Tams and scoff the lot before he even knows they're on offer.'

First child: 'I don't believe in discipline, or even saying anything critical, as it may crush his little spirit.'
Second child: 'We've adopted a time-out system, especially after the problem with the cigarette lighter.'
Third child: 'Come on, son, make my day. One more step and I use the capsicum spray.'

First child: 'We only allow him to watch BBC nature programs.'
Second child: 'We only allow him to watch nature programs and the odd episode of *Blue Heelers*.'
Third child: 'Hurry up, Trent, and bring the beer and nachos, you're missing the start of *The Sopranos*.'

First child: 'Each evening, we're going to read — as a family — for an hour.'
Second child: 'Sit and read where I can see you while I cook the dinner.'
Third child: 'You can tell those bloody teachers he reads the TV program *every bloody night*, so what's their problem?'

First child: 'Only when everybody is finished eating may you leave the table.'
Second child: 'You can jump up now but put your plate in the sink.'
Third child: 'Darren, stop wiping you hands on the couch. Use your T-shirt like your father.'

First child: 'I'm going to teach my child the value of money.'
Second child: 'I'll give you some pocket money if you stop crying.'
Third child: 'Fifty bucks and you don't tell Dad it was me who backed into his Commodore.'

First child: 'We try to limit it to nine or ten photographs each day, plus the odd bit of video filming.'
Second child: 'Those disposable cameras are great for capturing the really significant birthday parties.'
Third child: 'Of course we took photographs of you. Look at this photo of the dog — I'd swear that's your foot in the background.'

The real road rules

Batboy starts the car, puts it into gear and then tries to move off. It's our fifth driving lesson and things are not going well. The car does a couple of kangaroo hops and then shudders to a stop. He repeats the process another ten or twenty times. As his passenger, I'm developing the world's slowest case of whiplash. He tries again. The key. The gear. The clutch. The shuddering stop. Our bodies are thrown forward into our seatbelts and then thumped back into our seats. Would it affect the boy's confidence if I kitted myself out with a motorcycle helmet before our next driving lesson?

Slowly we stall our way along a little-used dirt road in the bush. Every time we shudder to a stop all the cows stop grazing and look up, their big moon eyes staring at us. 'Jeez Louise,' they seem to be saying, 'what is that boy doing to that car?' They give a baffled shake of their large heads and, with what looks like a sigh, return to their grazing. In all their years chewing cud by this roadside, they've never seen anything like it.

Maybe it's genetics. I took the best part of a year to learn to drive, taught by a series of kindly stepmothers. Luckily, my father ran through wives with such speed I could exhaust the patience of at least a couple.

Each stepmother would sit there in the passenger seat as I kangarooed down the driveway. Each time we'd stop, the relevant stepmother would turn and use her hands to describe what my feet should be doing. 'This foot goes down as this one comes up,' she would say, rotating her hands in opposite directions, like the wings of a dying seagull.

'How can that be?' I'd ask the stepmother. 'Why can't they make the car so that both pedals go in the same direction at the same time? It's like trying to pat your head at the same time as you rub your tummy. It's like they are *trying* to make it difficult.'

And so I'd start the engine and try to split my mind in two — the right brain focusing on the right foot, easing it down; the left brain focusing on the left, easing it up; before finally, in my confusion, pulling both feet off both pedals and shuddering to a halt in a blaze of bad language. I'd then exit the car, slam the door and start screaming at the vehicle, much in the manner of Basil Fawlty in *Fawlty Towers*.

In retrospect, it may not have been entirely my father's fault that he went through *quite* so many wives.

Finally I learnt to start the thing, only to find that this led inevitably to a series of fresh horrors. Such as learning to reverse — a kind of driving in which one turns the steering wheel in whatever direction seems most unlikely. Or reverse parking — a technique designed to ensure constant work for the panel beating industry.

Back on the bush track, Batboy finally triumphs over both the dodgy clutch and his dodgy genetics and gets the thing into first. We motor along for some metres and our mood lifts. It is then the road starts to wind upwards and I am forced to break the news about hill starts.

'So,' I say, repeating the speech of the stepmothers, 'you've got your right foot going down, the left foot coming up, and then at the same time you reach out with your hand and let the handbrake off.'

Batboy stares at me aghast. 'You've got to be joking. That's three completely separate things at the same time. That's just impossible.'

We give it a couple of goes but get nowhere. The car shudders backwards and forwards like a dying hippopotamus. Even the cows turn away their huge heads in a moment of embarrassment and contempt. We sit in the stalled car, both of us staring ahead into the gathering dusk.

It occurs to me that it would be less threatening if I went over the real road rules: not the ones taught in driving school but the road rules as practised by the appalling drivers you find in most Australian cities.

Rules like:

- The light turning yellow means accelerate.
- Once you turn your hazard lights on, you have the unfettered right to suddenly stop or park anywhere you like.
- Once you overtake someone on the freeway, you should slow down straight away so they understand how you felt being stuck behind them.

- If female, it's fine to put on your make-up while driving, including foundation, blusher, eyeliner and lip gloss. During tricky manoeuvres, such as crossing the Sydney Harbour Bridge, you may, however, like to go easy on the cucumber slices over the eyes.
- If male, remember your manhood is at stake every time the lights go green.
- A car with battered-in front and sides always gets right of way. The driver of this vehicle has proved that he is not easily deterred.
- If you are under twenty-five years of age, feel free to accelerate backwards out of your own driveway without looking. The music belting out of your sound system is considered warning enough.
- The time to turn on your indicator is *after* you've made a lane change; that way everyone knows you meant to make the shift and are not just weaving around aimlessly.
- If you are over eighty-five years of age, feel free to leave your indicator on permanently. When you finally turn left, it's reassuring to know that other road users have had a full three hours' warning.
- It's OK to use the breakdown lane on the expressway to avoid gridlocked traffic providing you are driving a late-model BMW. Other road users should realise that, with a car like that, you're a very important person and are late for a meeting more important than anyone else's.
- It's OK to park in a bus zone as long as you leave your windows open so everyone knows you're not going to be long.

- It's OK to go through a light just after it's turned red, although you are legally required to glance quickly and guiltily into the rear-view mirror just to make sure the police didn't see you.
- The bigger your four-wheel drive, the more right you have to ignore everyone else on the road.
- And never use a mobile phone while driving if you are also drinking a cup of coffee and smoking. Finish the cigarette first, as the ash could fall into your coffee, which might distract you from your call.

I weigh up whether to tell him these real rules and decide against. He seems to have enough problems right now without facing up to the fact that his fellow road users are quite insane.

After a few minutes' more silence, contemplating the hill ahead, Batboy mentions our friend Locky. He's a rice farmer down in the Riverina: the whole farm is completely flat, to the extent that he never has to use the handbrake. Locky simply pulls the ute to a stop, opens the door and gets out.

'Maybe I could get a job down there,' says Batboy, suddenly jettisoning all his complex career plans in favour of working somewhere *flat*.

I ask him to imagine the conversations he'll have in twenty years' time. 'So,' friends will ask, 'exactly why did you choose a career in the Australian rice industry? Was it through a desire to help the nation's exports or a passion to feed the world's hungry?'

'No,' he'll be forced to admit. 'The thing I really loved about the industry was the complete absence of hill starts.'

defiant

Here at Bloke, we either
solve problems or we deny
their existence. We
certainly never 'sit with'
them; that's for girls.

Ten ways to argue like a man

Everyone knows that men and women argue in different ways but can they be catalogued? Using a notebook, a tape recorder and a mirror, I've made a start cataloguing the male side of things. The list that follows is scarifyingly honest and personally embarrassing. Care should be taken that it doesn't fall into enemy hands. For example: Jocasta's.

1.   **There are no grey areas**. Your relationship is either the best relationship in the whole world; or it's a miserable farce. A wife should never attempt to suggest 'there's just one little thing that maybe we can improve', because the man will spot exactly what she is up to. She is kicking the chocks from beneath the wheels of the whole cart, thus sending it hurtling downhill. Remember, it's not what the wife is saying, it's what she is implying: 'What?

You'd like me to fetch the salad? So you're saying I'm lazy! That I do *nothing*! Well, I'm happy to cook the whole meal. I'll do it every night. On top of everything else. I'm surprised you're obviously so unhappy with our life together. You sound like you want a trial separation. And that may not be such a bad idea. I mean, considering the way you're talking.'

2. **Circular breathing**. In traditional Aboriginal society, the didgeridoo can only be played by men. That's because it involves circular breathing, in which one never pauses to draw breath — drawing air in from the side of the mouth as it is simultaneously expelled through the front. No wonder it's saved for the men: it's perfect practice for the male arguing style. The aim is to produce a constant stream of hectoring sound, thus preventing your opponent from ever slipping in a single word. Why not buy your bloke a didgeridoo this Christmas? You'll be amazed to find he can play it perfectly, first go. It's almost as if he's been practising for years.

3. **Everything you say is about him**. Your comment that 'I feel tired' is not just a general observation about the workplace, an ageing body and the end of the week. It's a hostile surprise attack on him and the life you've set up together. Naturally, he will deal with it as such. Two hours later, lady, and you're going to feel a lot more tired.

4. **Problems must be either solved or denied**. When you say 'My boss refused my pay rise', you may be

asking for a bit of sympathy, a moment when the two of you 'sit with' your disappointment. Well, honey, you've come to the wrong department. Here at Bloke, we either solve problems or we deny their existence. We certainly never 'sit with' them; that's for girls. Are you sure you asked for the pay rise in the right way? It may be your fault you didn't get it. Have you considered doing it in writing? On the other hand, would you like me to just go and hit the bastard?

5. **The importing of extraneous materials**. Some people when arguing say 'Stick to the point'. Trouble is you'll never win an argument that way. How to counter, for example, her stern observation that 'Last night, you drank most of a bottle of wine, plus three beers.' You could deny it (difficult, as the bottles are still there, sitting by the couch); you could apologise and promise never to do it again (demeaning and, besides, she's not *that* credulous); or you could move the argument to fresh turf. As in the example: 'Well, at least *my* uncle was never arrested for fraud.'

   Remember also, if drinking is the issue, that drinks are always spoken about in the singular but consumed in the multiple. 'Why don't you come over for a *drink*.' 'I thought I'd stay for a *drink*.' 'Well, maybe just one *drink*.' Just as the word 'sheep' can cover anything from one animal to a whole flock, so, once the drinking starts, can the single 'drink' metamorphose into seventeen beers and three red wines. Yet, remarkably, at the end of the process, it becomes a single drink again.

You've had 'just *one* drink too many'. If only you'd
left it at the seventeen beers and the *two* glasses of
red wine, you'd have been fine. When have you heard
a man admit the truth: 'I planned to stay for five
drinks, ended up having twelve and later realised this
was nine too many'?

6. **Never say sorry**. I'll rephrase that. Say sorry all the
    time, but with a range of inflections and modifiers
    that prove your 'sorry' is about as sincere as a closing-
    down sale at a Turkish rug shop. Classics include: 'I'm
    sorry . . . if you took it that way'; 'I'm willing to
    apologise . . . if it makes you feel better'; or, a
    personal favourite, 'OK, sure, I admit it, you're right
    and I'm the worst person in the world' (said in a voice
    so laden with irony that your vocal chords have
    trouble moving).

7. **Sigh.** The idea is to let loose the sigh at precisely the
    right volume so it can be heard distinctly and yet is
    still covered by the principle of plausible deniability.
    > 'Sighhhhhh.'
    > 'What's that supposed to mean?'
    > 'What?'
    > 'That sigh?'
    > 'What sigh?'
    > 'You clearly sighed.'
    > 'I think you must be imagining things, my dearest.'

8. **Sulk.** The real trick with sulking is to make sure it's
    noticed. There's nothing worse than putting in two or
    three days' hard sulking only to have your partner
    assume you are merely a little off-colour. Remember,
    one's aim is to hang around the house like a dark

cloud, an evil smell or, if you prefer, some sort of creeping fungal growth. If your partner seems oblivious to what you are up to, try humming appropriate tunes such as 'D.I.V.O.R.C.E.', or Smash Mouth's 'Pet Names' in order to draw her attention to the major sulk that is under way. Thus forcing the exchange:

'Hmmmmmm.'

'What's that supposed to mean?'

'What?'

'That sulking sound.'

'What sulking sound?'

'You're clearly sulking.'

'I think you must be imagining things, my dearest.'

9. **Play the martyr.** If sulking's not working for you why not try martyrdom? The trick is to paint your life as one of constant drone-like misery, thus making your partner feel guilty. Start with some menial tasks inside the house before moving outside in order to dig over the compost heap and then clean out a blocked sewage pipe or two. Try to cover most of your body in dirt and faecal matter before standing in full view of the window so she can see your dogged, saint-like behaviour. A halo of blowflies would help complete the intended tableau.

10. **The Final Word.** With the help of the methods above, men can usually survive most marital arguments, despite being less verbally skilled than women. They — *we* — should always, however, insist upon The Final Word, which involves standing back and shouting: 'I'm sick of arguing with you, you always

win, and not because you are in the right, but just because you argue better.' (Exit, down hallway, stomping.)

Sad to say, but it looks like your bloke has won yet another argument.

Up the mountain

It's been reported that over 1200 people have now climbed Mount Everest. Worse, a fair percentage have written a book about their experiences. These are not modest, wry books, such as those written by Sir Edmund Hillary. They are thumping, self-aggrandising tomes, in which the climber is always a self-sacrificing hero.

Well, maybe. But why can't someone put the same exciting spin on ordinary life. Staying at home. Looking after kids. Holding down a job over decades whether you enjoy it or not. Now *there's* heroism. Now *there's* self-sacrifice.

If only someone could write it up a little . . .

Many believe they've taken on an impossible feat, but Tracy and Steve Sweetbreath are adamant it can be done. Their aim: to live in Brisbane and raise two kids while avoiding bankruptcy, illegality or frothing insanity. Now in their early forties, the two of them believe they're at least halfway up the mountain.

'But that doesn't mean you can stop and celebrate,' says Tracy Sweetbreath, panting heavily as she hauls ten bags of shopping up her treacherously steep front steps. 'Some days, we really try to push forward. We make an assault on the mortgage; or search for a new approach that will take us around the Valley of Death that is my job. But most of the time it's a matter of just plodding forward. Trying not to drop your bundle.'

Tracy pauses, struggling to find her keys, while maintaining her hold on the shopping. 'Oh, for a team of Sherpas,' she jokes, grimacing as the plastic bags cut into her hands.

Tracy is aware that a dangerous storm could suddenly blow up, right out of nowhere, most likely in the form of Rowan, the Sweetbreath's teenage son. 'At the moment, we're trying to navigate our way through one of the most difficult sections of the whole ascent: the teenage years. There are sudden storms and many hidden pitfalls. There are also sections where everything gets very glacial. It's pretty hard to keep everyone on the same track.'

Inside the house Steve Sweetbreath is at base camp, preparing a meal of chops, potato and broccoli. 'Part of the problem,' he says, 'is that the ascent begins quite gently. You take on a house and a job, and for a while you score promotions and pay rises. You feel like you're getting somewhere. Then, sometime in your late thirties, the slope just becomes a whole lot steeper. You feel you're getting nowhere. Or even tumbling backwards. But by then you're committed to the climb.'

Steve throws some chops in the pan. 'I've had a few tumbles myself, as has Tracy. At certain times one of you will take a fall, drop down into some terrible dark abyss. And you just hope your grappling hooks are strong, and that you're tied to your partner in a way that holds. Quite a few times we've pulled each other out of the crevasse.'

From Steve's vantage point at the cooktop, he spots an argument building between Rowan and Tracy, the two of them standing at the doorway to Rowan's room. 'Classic hormonal storm,' observes Steve. 'Look how quickly it's growing in intensity. Tracy's tired from a day at work, battling uphill, virtually carrying her boss, year in and year out, and Rowan's suffering a testosterone blizzard. I'd go over and help but, frankly, it's too dangerous. No way do you want everyone standing on the same slippery slope. Better if I stay over here until the worst of it has passed.'

Will the climb get easier from now on?

'In some ways, yes,' says Steve. 'But your body starts to tire after the first forty years. And, as you plod on, you spot climbers who haven't made it. They've succumbed to the grog, or impatience, or rage. You see them bogged, unable to move forward.' Steve's voice drops to a pained whisper. 'I've even heard tell of those who leave their families and jobs and take up mountaineering or solo round-the-world yachting. It's sad.'

Over at the doorway, Rowan's hormonal storm has passed and there's a flash of smiles all round.

'No gain without pain,' grins Tracy. 'People say we are heroes but we're just doing what we love. Pitting ourselves against incredible odds.'

Steve agrees. 'On the positive side, Tracy and I have started giving motivational lectures. We'll have a roomful of people — say a conference of mountaineers or round-the-world sailors — and we'll just try to motivate them. A lot of them are amazed at our stories. These are people who've done challenges that last just a few weeks; at most a couple of months. They can't imagine sticking to one challenge over seventy or eighty years. Sometimes, when I'm telling our stories, I can see their eyes gleaming with excitement, realising how unchallenged they've been by their lives of endless mountaineering and drab adventuring. And it's those moments, I think, which make it all worthwhile.'

The Blokes' Supermarket

I see that Australian doctors are studying what they call 'oniomania', or the compulsive need to shop. I just wish they'd spare a thought for people like me who suffer from shopping reluctance, or to use the technical name 'tightwadmania'. All around I see my fellow citizens joyfully shopping, their gold Visa cards flashing festively in the sunlight, their shopping baskets full. Oh, that I could join them. Instead, I sit at home, fumbling for my wallet, only to find that my pockets are deep and my arms are short.

Everywhere I see barriers to my enjoyment of the shopping experience. For a start, have you seen the prices? Since when did a shirt cost $85 and a pair of daks $150? I feel as if I might faint were it not for the excessive price of smelling salts. Then there are the mirrors: they are everywhere. In a particularly cruel move, they've even put them into the changing rooms. How am I meant to convince myself to buy an $85 shirt when, right before me, is evidence of how appalling I look in it? Couldn't they borrow the mirror from Luna Park — the one that makes you tall and blessedly thin?

But most of all it's the excessive choice. How am I meant to know what style collar I want? Or which of the thirteen different kinds of jeans? How am I meant to know which of thirty-seven brands of ground coffee I should buy? Or how many pixels I want in a digital camera?

Shopping, already a complex activity, is getting worse with each passing week. In the supermarket down the road, they've added new specialty sections. Where's the olive oil? It could be in the Italian Section, in the Health Section, in the Gourmet Section or in Cooking Needs. It's probably in all four, since the idea is not to assist the shopper but to make you browse. By constantly shifting everything around, you are forced to walk through every aisle about twenty times, searching, looking, yearning.

There is now good evidence, I believe, that Coles and Woolworths are basing their store design on the ancient Cretan Labyrinth of the Minotaur. Vainly do we sacrifice seven youths and seven virgins to the management, yet they refuse to change the layout. And so, every day, you see shoppers unravelling balls of string just so they can find their way back from Dried Soup to Canned Fruit. No wonder they now open twenty-four hours; that's how long it takes to locate the Cheese Spread Snack Abouts.

I've long fantasised about a blokes' shopping mall, which would offer good parking, cheap prices and *really* minimal choice. The supermarket would offer only three products: lamb chops, beer and loo roll. They'd have a whole aisle each. No more trailing up and down the aisles, like the lost souls from Dante's Inferno, constantly bumping into the same lady, the one who insists on parking her trolley mid-aisle while she endlessly debates the choice between the freeze-dried carbonara or the freeze-dried puttanesca. Doesn't she realise they put the same salty goo into both packets?

In the Blokes' Supermarket, all of that hassle: gone. Into the trolley they'd go — lamb chops, beer and loo roll — and you'd be trundling on your way. The specialty vegetable shop would then beckon. 'Vegetables, sir?' the kindly assistant would holler from his shop doorway and, upon one's nod, a few head of broccoli, his only product, would be tossed into your cart. The practised shopper wouldn't even slow his trolley, simply signalling his thanks with a few accurately thrown coins.

At the bakery, there'd be a new product called the mixed loaf — a loaf of which one end would be white bread and the other wholemeal, with a kind of light rye in the middle. Adults could start eating at one end, the kids at the other, and everybody would be happy. I don't want to blow my own trumpet, but it would be the best invention since sliced bread. Using a small cannon-like device, the baker would lob a couple of loaves into your trolley as you trundled past; the charge billed to one's account.

With all this new efficiency, the shops would be able to drastically lower their prices, at last providing some relief to those members of the citizenry suffering from tightwadmania. With a little help and sympathy, one day our arms may even grow long enough to reach our wallets.

Style counsel

I've been looking through *In Style* magazine, which arrived the other day. Every couple of pages there's a profile of a Hollywood celebrity revealing his or her decorating tips. According to the magazine, every multimillionaire Hollywood star was born with innate style, which was displayed long before he or she became wealthy. The magazine doesn't disclose why, this being so, each has to hire a decorator to make every decision down to colour of the eggcups — but perhaps the celebs can't be bothered wasting their innate style on themselves.

For instance — I get this from the current issue — John Travolta lives in a fairly doozy pad in Los Angeles with his wife, Kelly Preston. Travolta gets paid $10 million to $20 million a picture, and has hired the decorator Christopher Boshears to rip out and refit the house. Yet it turns out neither Travolta's huge wealth nor the expertise of Mr

Boshears has any real bearing on the fact that his place now looks great. Travolta has innate style that doesn't require money.

Here's Travolta: 'My intent has always been to inspire others to do the same thing I'm doing, regardless of income, because I lived well when I had no money and also when I did have some money.'

At this point in the article, *In Style* quotes a friend cooing about the couple's 'aesthetic of living'. She says that Kelly, even when poor, would never drink out of a paper cup. Even if she could only afford to have one china cup, she would buy just one high-quality china cup. You can imagine dinner parties at their place: 'Hey, John, pass the wine would you and maybe I could have a go with the cup sometime soon? Plus how are you going with the knife and fork?'

The idea is that to possess humdrum Kmart objects reveals that you are a humdrum Kmart sort of person. It reflects not your income level but your very nature. The quality of the soul is divined through the possession of expensive objects. Not that I believe John or Kelly ever lived like this — with the one teacup and the one tasteful wine glass. It's a myth, of course, but one which seeks to underline the moral message: even a small income does not excuse any of us from buying stupidly expensive things. And how convenient that the advertisers are there on the next page to satisfy the hunger thus created.

The reality is that the person who fusses over the brand of their dinner plates or the quality of their glassware is generally a person without innate anything. Rather than 'stylish' and 'aesthetic' they are boring, shallow and materialistic. We all know this to be true, probably even the magazine's editors know it to be true. Yet if a magazine confessed the truth — that it is words and actions that tell you most about a person — its advertising would quickly dry up. 'Talk about interesting things! Read books! Be interested in other people! Be passionate about ideas!' Each is a useful slogan but not one that would lead to a lot of high-margin retail sales.

Truly interesting people don't have much time for objects at all, that's the truth of it. They don't decorate, other than shifting the couch every ten years, and they use cheap glassware with gay abandon.

Writing newspaper profiles, I used to spend days hanging out with various astounding people — writers, thinkers, activists, musicians. I rarely mentioned the brand names of the objects they possessed and wore because the objects were so ordinary. The truly fabulous are clothed by Target, with kitchenware by Kmart and a car by Toyota. Their favourite restaurant is the local Chinese. They don't care about the set design of their lives; they are interested in the downstage action.

In the face of the intimidating style-fascism of most magazines, I now regret that I didn't mention the mundane surroundings of those fabulous people. I may need to go back through some newspaper profiles and insert a few I-had-thought-obvious facts.

'Mr Mandela, wearing a 50/50 rayon/cotton mix shirt and black pants, purchased from an outlet whose name he can't recall, pulled a notepad from his pocket. Covered in genuine plastic, this useful pocket diary cost $4.99 at his local newsagency.'

Or this: 'The Australian poet Judith Wright throws open her kitchen cupboards. She has chosen Laminex doors, which have become charmingly distressed with the passage of time, and stocked the cupboards with an eclectic mixture of china and plastic, in which not one piece seems to match any other.'

'Was such a mixture planned by the feisty poet? "Not really," says the cardigan-wearing bard. "I've never noticed up to now."'

We could call it *Out of Style* magazine. We'd have less advertising but really fabulous profiles. And, after being inspired by the people within, you wouldn't feel the need to buy a thing — except for another copy of *Out of Style*.

Lip service

I don't know if you have noticed but the lips on American TV stars continue to grow bigger. On shows like *CSI* and *CSI Miami*, the lips now appear larger than the face onto which they are attached. With everything else immobilised by Botox, the actor has become a life-support system for the lips. Hollywood now awaits the birth of its dream woman: a woman with lips wider than her waist. It's the culture's way of saying: 'You see, I've got a mouth big enough to eat anything I like, but enough self-control to choose starvation.'

Go to an event like the Logies and it's like being at a Chupa Chups convention: everywhere the same body type — big head, big eyes, big mouth, all set onto a tiny, perfectly formed body. I went to the Logies a few years back and felt I should tread carefully, lest a couple of game show hosts be trampled underfoot. Wear a pair of open-toed sandals and you'd be picking out bits of weather presenter all night.

Already the TV stars remind me of Billy Bass, the battery-operated singing fish, in which nothing moves but a set of giant lips. Soon there'll be awards for the actress who can support her lips with the least visible strain. They already have the title: Best Supporting Actress.

Meanwhile, millions of people are using Botox, a paralysing agent which is injected into the face. Since the muscles are frozen, it becomes impossible to frown, and thus one's wrinkles begin to disappear. That's the idea. The question, though, is why you'd want a face that could no longer frown. George Orwell famously said that 'by fifty, everyone has the face they deserve', which presumably should now be rewritten: 'By fifty, everyone has the face they can afford.'

Personally, I love the subtleties of The Frown. Each frown is made up of a hatchwork of lines, mostly verticals and horizontals, yet their precise alignment can convey anything from aghast horror over politics to uncertainty about a piece of dodgy fish. This tiny ideogram, located in the centre of the forehead, has all the precision and eloquence you could hope for and is readable across cultures and generations. Imagine a spoken language that could do so much with such delicacy and in so tiny a space. And imagine, given such a language, that people would willingly render themselves mute. But that's the glory that is Botox.

Of course, the grass is always greener. If human beings had never developed The Frown, someone would have tried to. Imagine the advertisements on late-night TV: 'Amaze your friends. Learn how to express your emotions through your face. Tell a boyfriend he's not behaving properly without having to spell it out! Put the pressure on a child to do his homework without a big verbal showdown! All this could be yours with The Frown (copyright pending). Be among the first 300 callers and we'll also throw in instructions for The Dirty Look, The Glare and The Scowl.'

Part of the problem, of course, is that frowns leave marks. As do smiles, dirty looks and expressions of surprise. Thus Orwell's aphorism about having the face we deserve. Spend your life scowling — even in private — and in the end everyone will know your secret.

Not that I'm ruling out plastic surgery for myself. If God, or Charles Darwin, had done the job properly, all this fiddling around would not be necessary. I have long admired, for example, the concept of baby teeth. I love the way, at the age of six or seven, kids start to lose their baby teeth — and then get a whole fresh set. It's such a great idea. It's as if God, or Charles Darwin, realised that kids are not responsible enough to look after their first set of teeth and needed a second chance. You get one set of teeth to mistreat and misuse as a baby; then, when you've become a bit more responsible, you get a whole new set.

It's a good principle and one worthy of extension. I'd like to see God supply a third set of teeth, some time in late middle age: after all, even Ikea throws in a couple of extra bolts. With the maturity of my forties, I'd look after the third set. After that, God, or Darwin, could address the matter of our internal organs, in particular the liver. The new liver could be delivered around one's fortieth birthday. The Liver Fairy could drop two bucks on the bedside table and take the exhausted old one away.

A second chance with the belly would also be good. As with the teeth, you only start making an effort once you've got the problem. And by then it's too late. There's the moment, again in one's mid-forties, when the old belly starts to get a bit wobbly and loose. With a first tooth, that's the signal the old one's about to fall out. Same principle would work with bellies. Once it starts wobbling, you should be able to look forward to it coming loose and revealing the new flat belly below.

Slip the old one under your pillow and then the Belly Fairy would leave you two bucks and spirit the wretched thing away. It could then be sold to Hollywood for use in some Chupa Chups starlet's lips. Think about it: in a few weeks' time, your old beer belly could be locked in an embrace with Brad Pitt.

Recipe for disaster

Seventies food, I've been told, is making a comeback, with dishes like duck à l'orange and carpet-bag steak making regular appearances on restaurant menus. A couple of very fancy joints are even serving prawn cocktail — a dish that I assumed had been hunted to extinction by the early eighties. Yet if people want to recreate the authentic taste of the seventies, it's important to follow the rules of the time. It's no good just grabbing a recipe for steak Diane or apricot chicken; you've got to adopt the correct seventies sensibility.

This is where I come in: I was taught to cook by my father in the two days before I left home at the end of 1976 — the high point of seventies cuisine. The two recipes I learnt to prepare were steak Diane (for fancy) and Welsh rarebit (for day-to-day). I have flipped through some modern recipe books and none of the recipes as printed bears any relation to the way I was taught to do it.

Steak Diane, for instance, was far from being a complex dish involving cream, chopped parsley, cognac and garlic. Instead, it consisted of a piece of steak thrown in a frypan with a good wallop of Worcestershire sauce to finish. Welsh rarebit, far from being this thing involving milk, mustard, beer and a double boiler, was suspiciously similar to cheese on toast. 'Take the cheese, son, put it on the bread, then pop it under the griller,' my father would instruct, '. . . and *voilà*, Welsh rarebit.' My father's breakfast special — a raw egg cracked into a glass of milk and then swallowed as one rushed out the door — was similarly dignified by the term 'eggnog'.

Another problem. Modern cookbooks blather on about 'using the freshest ingredients possible', but this was not the authentic seventies way. The steak, for a start, had to be frozen and then defrosted. For reasons that now remain unclear, everyone was absolutely crazy about buying meat in bulk and then freezing it. If you didn't have half a cow slung in a chest freezer in the laundry, you hadn't really made it. You could have butcher shops on either side of you, and you'd still buy three months' worth of meat at a time and store it under a mountain of frozen peas and beans, as if you were living on the outer Barcoo.

Meanwhile, for reasons which again remain unclear, both potatoes and sweet corn were cooked in the oven wrapped in aluminium foil. 'We can't afford to have the house clad in aluminium but at least we can clad the spuds' — that was the line of thinking.

Over at the house of my school friends, things were even more sophisticated, if that's possible. Many and varied were my encounters with the canned pineapple piece. The rule seemed to be: when in doubt, toss in a can-full, whether it's dessert, main course, breakfast or lunch. I try as I write to fight off memories of the lamb chops with pineapple sauce served regularly at one friend's house.

After I'd completed my father's two-day cooking course, I set out for my new home, the garage out the back of a friend's place. Two weeks later, I realised my diet consisted of nothing but steak, cheese and Worcestershire sauce. Alarmed that death might be imminent, I acquired a copy of *The Vegetarian Epicure* — a book which consisted of a hundred recipes in which one would take some form of vegetable matter and then dump half a ton of cheese on it. With particularly disgusting vegetables, more complex recipes were required, in which you would make sure the vegetable was dead by further drowning it in sour cream.

As the years went on, things became ever-more stylish. I particularly remember the great Cooking-at-the-Table boom of 1977, in which butane burners were placed on the tabletop. All manner of fondues and dishes of browned bananas were prepared, much to the delight of everyone, normally with Cat Stevens' *Tea for the Tillerman* playing on a stereo nearby.

But, of course, every golden period must come to an end. People got rid of their chest freezers after a spate of power blackouts resulted in them having to eat a whole cow over a couple of sittings — a task that could really do in one's supplies of Worcestershire sauce. And the Cooking-at-the-Table boom ended after some very nasty incidents involving nylon body-shirts, ruffled chest hair and bottled gas.

Last to go was the moulded, gelatinous fish dish, made in the shape of a fish. Someone — history has lost the name —

came up with the idea that, instead of dismembering the fish, chopping it up, adding sour cream and powdered gelatine, and then moulding it all back into a fish shape, you could try just serving the fish.

And with that startling insight the seventies were dead. Oh, happy day that they may now be coming back, led by the mighty prawn cocktail. Bags the first chest freezer of the new run.

The Christmas cheer

In the shopping centre car park I am hunting shoppers. I spot a young bloke pushing a trolley and start following him, like a lion stalking a limping antelope. I become very proprietorial. This is my shopper and already his parking space is mine. I creep a bit closer, just to make sure our relationship is clear to other drivers. By the time I'm finished, I'm nosing along three centimetres away from his legs. If he stops suddenly I'll run him over. But the season of goodwill requires some sacrifices.

As it happens, I've chosen the one shopper who gets to his car, jumps in and then makes fifteen mobile phone calls. He's a parking tease, almost as bad as the elderly couples who get into their cars and then just sit there, looking smug. People like this should be compelled to wear a large sign and perhaps ring some sort of bell. Heavy of heart, I pick out another victim.

I've only come here to escape the house. Christmas cards are arriving in batches from Jocasta's old boyfriends, reporting another year of economic and social triumph.

'Oh,' says Jocasta, leafing through the stack, 'Tim says to say hello. He's just won the Nobel Prize for Physics.' All Tim's children, it appears, have had not a minute to spare between receiving academic honours and being feted with sporting prizes. His wife has enjoyed a series of pay rises to the extent that her salary now dwarfs the GDP of several small African nations. 'They are all just back from a European holiday,' says Jocasta. She reads out loud a terribly witty description of Prague in the autumn. 'He was always such a good writer,' sighs Jocasta, staring at the card with a sort of transfixed fondness.

Back in the car, I fiddle with the radio. One station is playing 'Chestnuts Roasting on an Open Fire', which is a fairly accurate description of the temperature inside the car. I'm guessing Tim's has airconditioning that works. My aim is to buy a present for Batboy, a teenager with no interests outside soccer and World War II Soviet history, and a gift for my mother, a woman whose interests include germ eradication and tormenting her only son. I figure I can be in and out of here in half an hour, providing Target sells a soccer shirt with Stalin decals, and Spray n'Wipe does some sort of gift pack.

Steering around a corner in the car park, I spot a twenty-year-old woman with a trolley and scoot behind her. She looks frantic and exhausted; a broken woman. Good. She won't muck around once she gets to her car. The trolley-pusher slumps into her car, speeds off and I nose into the space. Soon I'll look as shattered as her.

Inside the mall, people are shoulder to shoulder, staggering under the weight of perfumed, extruded and overpriced tosh. Some are hovering over the gift displays, a desperate look in their eyes, wondering by what leap of logic they can link any of this packaged crap to their Auntie June. That's the point — you're meant to give the present, then say something that indicates personal knowledge.

A golfing ashtray? 'I remembered you once played golf.' A pair of socks? 'I noticed you still had both your feet.' A gift pack of soaps? 'I couldn't help focusing, last time we met, on your shocking personal odour.'

Certainly, people are *desperate* to buy. They heave themselves at displays of fancy soap like Russians in a bread riot. All the soaps have got these girly-posh names like Evelyn and Trilby, or Figtree and Algernon, but there's nothing girly-posh about the shopping style. I see one lady charge through the crowd and grab hold of a gift pack of Somerset and Stevens Lavender Infusion, before letting loose a little yelp of triumph. 'That's Auntie Annabelle *done*!' she exclaims to her friend, using the word 'done' in much the same tone as a Mafia hit man admiring his latest bloodied corpse.

Not that I'm being critical. I know the feeling. You trudge through crowds hoping that the perfect gift will suddenly materialise before your eyes. The problem of Uncle Steve or young Cousin Trish is so intractable, so beyond all human understanding, that you can't bear thinking about it. You try to focus on it but the mind is unwilling: it just keeps shying away, like a horse unwilling to attempt a particularly difficult jump. Far better, you decide, to wander aimlessly until something suggests itself. You walk through the aisles, eyes flicking from side to side, as if the perfect present will just suddenly throw itself into your path. 'I'm here,' a tea-caddie will yell, leaping to the floor and doing handsprings. 'She loves tea, remember?' Or: 'Look here,' a cat calendar will say, purring about your legs as it unfurls its pages. 'Didn't she once have a cat?'

The result, some three hours later, is a desperation so intense and palpable that almost everything starts to look like the perfect present.

Kitty litter? Well, she does have a cat and if I wrapped it prettily . . . Handkerchiefs? Well, last Christmas she had a rather disgusting cold . . . A skateboard? Actually a lot of people in their eighties take it up . . .

I've seen the desperation from both sides of the counter. Working as a teenager in my father's newsagency during the week before Christmas, I would see people queuing up and down the shop with great piles of merchandise in their arms, picking up more from the stands as they waited. Every time they picked up a product, they could cross a name off their list. And so keen were they to cross off names, they hardly even looked at what they were picking up.

'Surely young James would like a Yugoslav news magazine,' you could see them thinking as they added a well-thumbed copy of *Nedeljni Telegraf* to their pile. Or: 'I think anyone, however old, can use a protractor and compass set.' Or: 'This set of five rolls of masking tape would be an excellent surprise.' My father would glance up at the waiting crowd, as we raced to take their money. 'You could sell 'em buckets of sand tonight,' he would mumble in wonderment, as we threw some more coins in the till.

Back at the mall, my fear is rising that I won't find anything. I recall that, according to Jocasta, her old boyfriend Tim does all his shopping by the internet. 'He says it's easier but then he's very good with computers.' I ask at Target if they've got anything featuring Red Army generals suitable for a teenage boy but draw a blank. Unbelievably, Spray n'Wipe doesn't do a gift pack.

Hours have passed and I'm close to defeat. Things are so bad, I enter the surf shop — a place where the prices have long lost any connection with reality. I emerge, bankrupted, with a good present for Batboy and something totally inappropriate for my mother — a pair of jewelled rubber thongs with the legend 'Surf Bitch'. My mother, of course, will view the gift as further evidence of her son's rising insanity, combining bad language, bad taste and the filthiness that is the wearing of thongs.

'You realise,' says Jocasta, when I finally get home, 'she'll blame me for not getting something good. And she'll mention it for years and years and years.' I smile to myself. Rather like Jocasta keeps mentioning Tim.

It's great at Christmas to come up with the present that just keeps on giving.

A night's tale

Back in the year 2000, I had some passing success with a book I published under the title *In Bed with Jocasta*. Now I fear I must recall all the copies and change the title. *No Longer in Bed with Jocasta* would be more accurate. Three or four nights out of seven I am asked to leave the marital bed. The method of request is a series of violent attacks, staged without warning, in the dark, and from behind. By the time Jocasta is finished, I feel I'm suffering from shaken husband syndrome.

Jocasta's complaints include my teeth-grinding, my wriggling and, most of all, my snoring. I feel pretty sure these are all a figment of her imagination, as I've never heard myself snore. Uncharitably, she imitates me, making a sound that is a cross between a dying wildebeest and a bearded seal in the last moments of lovemaking.

On the nights I manage to maintain my position in the bed, I have to endure a detailed report card in the morning.

'How did you sleep?' I ask chirpily. 'Only average,' says Jocasta. 'You snored for the first hour, ground your teeth for the next three and then fell into a sort of fitful snorting.'

She makes me sound so attractive.

'Exactly what were you grinding in there,' she then goes on to ask, 'corn supplies for the Mexican army? It just went on and on and on. Did you complete their order?'

I put forward the theory that it's just the tension of living with her, at which point she picks up my empty red wine bottle from the night before and pointedly flings it in the recycling. 'Maybe it's me but maybe it's something else,' is all she says.

She's torn out an article from the *Sydney Morning Herald*. It's by Adele Horin, the paper's resident feminist, and it details some British research. Every woman with a husband over forty discloses she has a problem with her partner's snoring. By contrast, according to the article, the women themselves are mostly perfect — indulging in little more than occasional ladylike gurgling.

The statistics seem pretty watertight, so I go for the *ad hominem* attack. 'You mean old snorter Horin? No wonder she's interested in sleep research. Every time she nods off, the whole neighbourhood knows about it. She lives under the flightpath but still you can hear every snort. With her, it's the airlines who ring the hotline number to complain about the noise. Apparently she keeps waking people on the overnight to Singapore.'

Jocasta looks unimpressed. She describes Adele Horin as 'my favourite journalist by far'.

The next night she makes me wear a mouthguard provided by the dentist to minimise teeth-grinding. It makes me ever more attractive. As I slot it into my mouth, it makes a wet clunking noise, like a gumboot slipping into mud. There is another sound. That of Jocasta shimmying over to the most distant edge of the bed.

The Thing works by holding my mouth slightly open so I look like a startled trout. It also encourages a sort of gurgling noise as I fall off to sleep. The huddled shape on the other side of the bed lets loose a small shudder of disgust. She's got a point. The Thing makes me sound like a toothless drunk with a spittle problem.

'What are you doing now,' bleats Jocasta, finally turning towards me, 'making coffee? Did the Mexicans need something to wash down the corn bread?'

Tenderly, I rub her back. 'Shorry, if I'm shopping you shleeping. I'm trying to go to shleep myshelf.'

But shleep is hard to achieve. The Thing lies with evil intent in my mouth. Why can't I just stop grinding? I stopped myself smoking by gritting my teeth, but it's harder now the problem is that I grit my teeth. Perhaps a cigarette would help?

I start to nod off but I'm beset with fears that Jocasta may be about to push me out of the bed. I keep having falling dreams, right there in the borderland between sleep and wakefulness. I feel myself being pushed off a cliff, only to look back as I fall and see Jocasta standing there at the top laughing. Just before I hit the bottom, my body is caught by this huge involuntary spasm, my legs shooting out as if hit by a doctor's hammer, thumping into Jocasta's body. 'Marvellous,' she mumbles, 'the nightly repertoire grows ever larger. What next? Star jumps? A *Son et Lumière* display? A haka?'

In the morning I re-read the piece from the *Herald*. According to Snorter Horin, men feel very sensitive about leaving the marital bed. Not me. I admit defeat, I gather up my books, mouthguard, Ventolin and water glass, and install myself in the spare bedroom. That night I sleep like a baby. That is, I wake up at about three in the morning, feel like bawling and then crawl up the hallway and into the main bed.

In deference to Jocasta, I slip the mouthguard back in with the usual wet clunking sound. 'Shorry,' I say. 'Shomehow I felt a bit lonely and shad.'

Jocasta says it's pathetic and I should be ashamed of myself. Still, my snoring was so loud she could hear it from three rooms away so I may as well sleep next to her. In the dark I rejoice with a secretive smile of victory and fall into a blissful shleep. I won't need to reissue the old book; not yet anyway. Miraculously, all these years later, I'm still in bed with Jocasta.

Richard Glover

'Richard Glover
is a renaissance man;
intelligent, witty,
insightful, wise . . .
and fabulous
in pantaloons.'
GRETEL KILLEEN,
author of *Visible Panty Line*

In Bed
with
Jocasta

IN BED WITH JOCASTA

'I first met Jocasta when I was twenty-one. I was pimply and unattractive and she did things in bed that no other woman was willing to do. For instance: staying *in* the bed when I hopped into it . . .'

For better for worse, in sickness and in health, in car park and shopping mall, this may be the world's weirdest love-story.

'I have spent many years trying to convince the newspaper-reading public of Jocasta's unfair ways and fierce nature. Alas, she grows more popular with her every outrage. Women, I'm told, have taken to quoting her behaviour, with some suggesting she is some sort of *go-girl* role model. Hopefully, with the length afforded by a book, I can finally white-ant this emerging fan base, and fully catalogue her crimes.'

'This ain't Proust.'
— Matt Condon, *Sun-Herald*

'Glover is better than Proust. OK, maybe not better, but how often do you find yourself in a cold bath at midnight still chuckling over Proust?'
— Debra Adelaide, *Sydney Morning Herald*